Stray

Kai's Story

AMBER D. LEWIS

For all the lone wolves looking for their pack.
Welcome Home.

ALSO BY AMBER D. LEWIS
RECOMMENDED READING ORDER

THE NIGHT THE STARS FELL

SCARS: ALAK'S STORY

THE STARLIGHT IN THE SHADOWS

STAR-CROSSED: CAL'S STORY

THE STARDUST IN THE ASHES

STRAY: KAI'S STORY

Author Note

This story includes some material that may be upsetting for some readers, including death, grief, mourning, and learning to move past that grief.

One character is drugged without consent to inhibit his fighting abilities; however, there is no sexual assault (or sex of any kind) anywhere in this book.

Animals (human shifters in their animal forms) are wounded and killed, but the descriptions are not overtly graphic.

ONE

I race through the trees, following the cheerful laugh ringing in the air. I don't even bother holding back my grin as I catch a glimpse of Leyana through the trees. She's not nearly as far ahead as she thinks. Her laugh carries on the wind and I smile. I know where she's going.

I cut through the trees on my left and head to a small dropoff, leaping the distance with ease before swinging back around and heading toward town. Sure enough, right as I reach the path, Leyana breaks through the trees. She doesn't see me at first, her head turned to look over her shoulder. When she turns her eyes ahead, they widen as they fall on me. She laughs and spins, ready to run off in the opposite direction, but I reach her in three quick strides, looping my arms around her waist.

"Told you I'm impossible to outrun!" I crow, lifting her off the ground as she laughs and twists in my grip.

"One day, Kai!" she gasps between giggles. "One day I'll outrun you!"

I set her on the ground and she looks up at me, her eyes bright. "Did the run work to clear your head?"

I nod, a smile playing on my lips. "Yeah, I think it did."

"Good," she says, bouncing back toward town, "because I'm starving and I bet Gaiya has something delicious for lunch."

I join her stride for stride as we follow the worn path into town. Our village of Nara in the Aleahya Province of Gleador is small and intimate. We boast no more than 500 citizens, and we all know each other fairly well. We're one big family. So I know something is off when the people we pass avoid meeting my eyes. When I glance over my shoulder after walking past them, their gazes linger, further unsettling me.

"Ley," I start, my attention focused on one man who's watching me like he's expecting me to break at any moment. "Maybe we should—"

"Why are there so many people outside our house?" Leyana cuts me short.

My gaze snaps ahead to the crowd that is indeed gathering outside the dwelling we call home. At least a third of the crowd seems drawn here, and their expressions are far too somber to be comforting.

"Leyana, maybe you should—"

She's off, racing toward our house before I can stop her.

"Leyana!" I yell, chasing after her.

But it's too late. She's already elbowing her way through the crowd, many of the villagers moving aside to give her a clear path. I'm only a step behind her, but she still sees the scene first. A shrill cry escapes her lips and she spins around, crashing into me and burying her face in my chest with a sob. Dread is heavy in my chest as I look inside.

Gaiya, our surrogate mother for all intents and purposes, lies face down in the center of the room in a puddle of her own blood, her limbs twisted in a way that isn't natural. My stomach lurches and bile rises in my throat as the coppery scent of the blood floods my nostrils. The shock is quickly replaced by rage. My eyes flick around the room. It's in disarray. Papers and books lay scattered around amongst broken pottery. Who did this? Who invaded my home? Who dared breach our trust? My rage rises so high I can barely see.

A sob breaks me from my thoughts and I wrap my arms around Leyana, squeezing her closer. She sobs again, clutching my shirt in her hands. I press a quick kiss to the top of her head. I need to get her out of here. I quickly scan the crowd, my eyes landing on the concerned face of Mistress Polliana, the mother of one of Leyana's closest friends. She meets my gaze and nods once.

"Leyana," I whisper, pulling her back away enough so she can look up at me. "Come."

She nods and allows me to steer her through the crowd. Once we're close, Polliana extends her arms and I allow her to take Leyana from me, though it takes a great push of my will to fight my instincts to keep Leyana where I can see her.

"Come, dear," Polliana soothes, wrapping her arm around Leyana's shoulders. "Let's get you some tea, yes?"

Leyana nods but casts a glance over her shoulder at me. I swallow hard but manage what I hope is an encouraging smile.

"Go on. I'll take care of things and fetch you when I'm done."

Leyana hesitates a moment before she nods and allows Polliana to lead her away. Once she's out of hearing range, I storm back toward our home.

"What happened?" I yell, scanning the crowd.

Most of the people shrug, avoiding my eyes as they look to each other.

"Someone had to see something," I push, forcing a few people to meet my eye. "What the hell happened?"

"There was an attempted robbery," an easy voice carries over the mumbles of the crowd.

I spin and search for the voice's owner and spot my close friend Nova elbowing their way through the crowd toward me. They stop a few feet away, their eyes bloodshot and cheeks damp with tears.

"A robbery?" I ask. "What did they hope to steal from Gaiya?"

Nova's jaw tightens as they glance around, hesitating.

"Well?"

They sigh and place a hand on my arm. I flinch under their touch but don't pull away.

"Let's discuss it out of the range of all these ears, huh?" they say, giving my arm a gentle tug.

I don't want to wait; I want to know now. The tight expression on Nova's face has me considering otherwise. I manage a sharp nod.

"Good. Follow me."

They release my arm and I fall into step beside them as we leave the crowd behind. Once we're alone, Nova veers over to a narrow pass between two houses where we can talk undisturbed.

"The thief was after this." They reach into their vest pocket and withdraw a small brown leather-bound journal. I inhale sharply as I snatch it from their grasp. "I take it you recognize it?"

I nod, my heart rate picking up. "It belonged to my mother." I jerk my eyes over to Nova. "You didn't—"

Nova cuts me off with a wave of their hand, shaking their head. "No. I recognized it as yours right away." They pause, eyeing the journal in my hand. "Though I was curious what would draw a thief to steal it. It doesn't look like much."

I shake my head, opening the journal to thumb through its pages. "It's all useless history and speculation. Nothing worth stealing." I pause, my eyes catching on a rough sketch of a wolf. Nova follows my gaze and I snap the journal shut. "It's a record kept by my great-grandfather. Nothing more."

Nova nods, not looking entirely convinced.

"Where is the thief now?"

"Taken to the magistrate to be served justice."

"Thank you."

I spin and stride toward the magistrate's office, located in the center of our village.

"Wait! Kai!" Nova calls, bounding after me. "Let them handle it."

I turn a sharp glare to Nova that has them shrinking back, but I don't slow my gait. "Someone attacked my family, and that cannot stand."

"I know. Trust me, I know. But that doesn't mean you can barge in and interrupt the process."

"The process?" I spit. "The process can go to hell."

"Kai, stop." Nova skirts in front of me, coming to a halt as they hold their hands up.

I growl and try to move around them, but they're quicker.

"Let me by, Nova."

They shake their head. "Look, I know you want justice, maybe even vengeance, but if you barge in there, Magistrate Fenbrook will have your head. You're not on his good side. Let me go in and observe everything. He likes me. When I have solid information, I'll come fetch you. Okay?"

"And what should I do in the meantime?"

"Go and take care of the body," Nova says softly, placing a gentle hand on my arm. "Then go take care of your sister."

Leyana. I glance over my shoulder toward where Polliana's house sits. I should go to her. I sigh, shaking my head.

"It's not fair she has to go through this," I whisper, more to myself than to Nova. "She's already lost one mother, although she was too young to truly know her. She remembers bits of our father though. No one should have to bear that much loss."

Nova gives my arm a small squeeze. "You've been through that loss as well, Kai. Only it's worse for you because you remember."

I swallow and nod, my chest suddenly heavy. "You would think it gets easier but . . ."

Nova nods knowingly. "But it doesn't, not really. Grief rarely vanishes entirely; it only changes form. Now, go on. Take care of the things that need attending."

I meet Nova's eyes. "And you swear you'll come get me when I can see this thief, look them in the eye?"

Nova nods. "I swear on the life of my own mother." They give me a slight push. "Now, go."

TWO

I wake with a jerk, the cold seeping in around me despite the layers of blankets I'm buried under. I blink, clearing my head of the haze of sleep, and push back my blankets. I don't remember my dream, but it's left me feeling uneasy.

I rise from the small cot in the corner and survey the rest of the single-room house where I'm staying. My host is already gone for the day it seems, but he shouldn't be hard to find. I quickly dress in warm layers, making sure I have Queen Khristiana's gold emblem looped around my neck on its chain.

When Queen Khristiana came to Callenia asking for help with a rogue shifter in exchange for her aid in the war, I accepted. I didn't much like leaving Astra behind, but she had Ronan, and the others likely returned not long after I left. When I saw an opportunity to help, I couldn't say no.

I stayed with the queen and her entourage until we passed into Paravlia. The queen gave me her blessing, along with her crest so people would know I was in service with her, and sent me on my way to find the shifter Hammon. I appreciated being able to work alone without her soldiers looking over my shoulder. I work best alone.

I push aside the thick fur serving as a door and step outside, the biting wind assaulting me immediately. I grumble to myself and pull my wool cloak closer, but it barely does anything against the cold. I trudge toward the center of town in search of my host, Pavel. He's one of the few who speaks Common Paravlian, the dialect I'm familiar with, so I tend to stick closely to him.

I find him at the altars, paying his respects to the patron gods of his village, or as the locals call it, his *orta*. *Orta* was a word I had only heard in passing before. When Queen Khristiana came to Callenia to recruit me, she used the word "tribe," but I've come discover the word translates more closely to "family" or "kinship." The particularly dense and rough terrain of Paravlia makes travel difficult in some regions, creating pockets of people smaller and more intimate than a typical village.

Even though the next *orta* may only be a matter of hours away on foot and they all follow the law given to them by the ruling monarch of Paravlia, they're each unique with their own rules and regulations based on the patron gods they choose to serve. These gods each have an altar placed in a central location that, to the common, uneducated eye, looks like little more than towers of eight-foot stones. On closer inspection, however, one sees the intricate symbols and words carved painstakingly into each stone, giving honor to the gods.

I stand off to the side, allowing Pavel his privacy as he kneels and prays before the altars, but I catch his eye as he passes from one altar to another. He offers me a small smile and a nod before continuing his prayers and acts of devotion. When he finishes his final prayer, he heads my way, a wide smile on his face.

"Morning, friend," he says, placing a hand on my shoulder. I tense under his touch but don't pull away. "Did you sleep well?"

I nod. "Well enough."

"Good. Good." He glances around before adding, "I have good news. The woman you have been waiting for arrived last night."

I perk up at his words, looking around eagerly. "Where is she?"

Pavel chuckles, shaking his head. "When I say 'last night' what I really mean is 'early this morning.' She is still asleep, and we should leave her that way."

I growl. "I don't have time to play waiting games."

"Look, friend, I know Eleni and if you wake her before she is ready to start her day, she will bite your head off and refuse to help you on principle. It's best to allow her time. Now, come and get breakfast with me while we wait."

The urge to argue and insist he take me to Eleni, a shifter who supposedly has information about Hammon, rises, but I push it down with a sigh. He knows her better than I do, and from what I've already heard, she's . . . difficult. I need to do everything I can to win her over. I reluctantly follow Pavel over to a bonfire a few yards away. The other men around the fire greet Pavel with enthusiastic words and me with polite nods of recognition. I'm offered a mug of freshly brewed coffee and a bowl of porridge with a side of toast. As they eat, they chatter away in one of the dialects of Paravlian I don't know, so I only catch the occasional word here and there.

My breakfast is long finished when I sense her.

When I first arrived, I knew without a doubt that among their tight-knit *orta* of roughly 300 people, 32 of them were shifters, and of that 32 only 5 were wolves. But now my senses are on full alert, preparing for a threat. I twist around and lock eyes with a young woman in her mid-twenties. She's tall and lithe with a fierce expression that would immediately ward off anyone with common sense. Her skin is a lighter shade of brown than is common in Paravlia, but still darker than what is common in Gleador. She raises her lip in a sneer that, were she in her wolf form, might have been a snarl or warning growl.

"Ah, yes, that's her—Eleni," Pavel says, drawing my attention. He stands, brushing off his pants. "Let me introduce you."

Pavel leads me over. The closer we get, the more I fear she'll lunge forward and rip out my throat. I'm prepared for any attack when we stop in front of her.

"Did you sleep well, Eleni?" Pavel asks, using the dialect I'm familiar with mostly for my benefit.

The corners of her mouth tip up in something that could almost be considered a smile if there wasn't something so deadly about it. "I suppose." Her eyes flick to me. "Who are you?"

"This is—" Pavel starts.

"No," Eleni says sharply, waving her hand. "I wasn't asking you. I was asking *him.*"

"I'm Kai." I don't bother extending my hand. I have a feeling she would be more likely to bite it off than shake it.

She crosses her arms and takes me in from head to toe.

"You're the ambassador from Callenia?"

"I am."

"And yet you're not from Callenia."

"I . . . How do you know?"

Her lips curl up into a more devious grin and I realize with a start she switched to Gleador at some point and I didn't catch it.

"Yes, I am from Gleador. I grew up in the Aleahya Province but have spent the last several years in the Hundan Valley."

She waves her hand. "I don't need your full backstory, wolf."

I grind my teeth and huff through my nose.

"What I do need is for you to go away and leave me be."

"I need your help."

"I know. I've been told. And I have no desire to lead you to your death."

I scoff and her eyes narrow.

"Oh, you think you're better than all the others who have tried to go against Hammon?"

I cross my arms. "Maybe."

Pavel clears his throat next to me and I nearly jump. I had forgotten he was there.

"Well," he says in Paravlian, glancing from me to Eleni and back again. "I'll leave you to discuss things."

He bounds off before either Eleni or I can protest, not that I suspect either of us would. Eleni sighs and starts to walk off in the opposite direction, but I lunge ahead and cut her off.

"I need your help," I grind out, emphasizing each word.

"And I said no," she says, matching my tone.

I pull the queen's emblem from my pocket and hold it up for her to see. "Your queen has—"

"No," she snaps, cutting me short. "Your jewelry means nothing to me. The queen of Paravlia is not your queen and therefore her permission, guidance, whatever you want to call it, means nothing to me or to you."

"Look, my fam—my friends and their kingdom are in danger. I need to do what I can to help them. I need to protect them, and I need your assistance to do that."

She narrows her eyes. "What's in it for me if I help you?"

I pause, thinking for a moment. "What do you want?"

She grins and there's something very wolfish about it. "A favor."

"What sort of favor?"

She lifts a shoulder in a half shrug, her grin holding strong. "I don't have an immediate need. You can just owe me a favor to collect on later."

I clench my jaw. Anyone with common sense knows not to enter a deal like this, but I'm desperate. I've been searching for over a week to find information about Hammon, and Eleni may be my only lead to reach him and take him down.

"Fine."

She thrusts her hand out to me. "Shake on it?"

I grab her hand harder than necessary and shake.

"Excellent," she says, pulling her hand away. "Let's go for a walk."

She leads me out of the settled part of the *orta* where we can talk well out of the range of prying ears. She spins around to face me so abruptly I nearly plow into her.

"You can't take Hammon down," she states simply, crossing her arms. "He's unstoppable and you'd be a fool to try."

I shake my head. "I plan on trying anyway. The more information you can give me, the better chance I have at surviving."

"No, you don't understand. You *cannot* beat him. Even with what information I have, and I have more than most."

"Why don't you leave that up to me?"

She laughs but it's humorless. "Fine. You want to play the part of the fool, so be it." She turns on her heel and marches off, heading into the woods surrounding the *orta*. "What is it you want to know?"

"The list is long," I say, falling into step beside her. "Let's start with how he came to power so quickly. I know he has a brother who's in a position of power, but beyond that I don't fully understand how he gained ground so effortlessly."

"His brother, Gerand, may be the one with the position in

the public eye, but it's always been Hammon running things. His brother is but his puppet. And they're half-brothers, anyway. Hammon is the bastard son of their father. Gerand had all the name and influence and Hammon had the mind for politics."

I nod, mulling her words over. "So Hammon has really been the one in charge the whole time?"

Eleni shrugs. "More or less."

"So what made him take the leap for more power?"

"Magic. Hammon has it and Gerand does not. There was a void in what Gerand could offer those with magic and Hammon filled that void without hesitation. Hammon may be evil, but he's charismatic. When magic popped up, his brother was floundering trying to figure out how to handle it. Hammon was quick to step into position and offer hope and encouragement to those with magic, especially other shifters. By the time people figured what he was up to, it was too late."

I frown. "What was he up to?"

Eleni hesitates, selecting her next words carefully. "The dangerous thing about Hammon isn't that he's simply hungry for power. He's clever and very intelligent. The moment magic returned he found every magical text he could and researched it thoroughly. Nothing was too dark for him to consider." She comes to a stop, meeting my eyes. "He discovered blood magic."

I inhale sharply. I know that not all blood magic is bad—Astra and Alak's own soul bond is tied together with blood magic—but it is strong magic. The strongest, really, which makes it practically unbreakable. It's the magic that was twisted to create the Dragkonians and part of what makes them unbeatable. Eleni takes in my reaction, likely assuming that I not only know how powerful the magic is, but that I also believe it's always dark.

"I know. People started coming to him for guidance and he acted like a kind benefactor. What he was really doing was binding everyone to him through ancient blood spells. He took advantage of everyone's desperation to control them."

She starts walking again, ducking under a low-hanging branch. I dive after her.

"I understand how that worked at first, but once word got out about the blood magic, why didn't people stop making deals with him?"

"He's clever, remember?" She glances at me over her shoulder. "He knew people would do anything if he had the right leverage. He went after the weakest and most vulnerable, tricked them into the blood oaths. Then the wiser of those left had little to no choice to join him as well."

It takes me a moment to read between the words, to figure out what she's saying. When realization strikes, my eyes widen and a growl escapes my throat.

"Children. He went after children."

"And we have a winner!" Eleni declares, throwing her arms wide, but there's no amusement in her voice.

"Even more of a reason he should be taken down."

Eleni sighs and spins around to face me. "I know he needs to be taken down. I never said he didn't. It just isn't possible for one wolf to do it."

"You don't even know me."

"I don't need to know you to know you'll fail. Just like the dozens of shifters before you. He can't be beat."

"You don't—"

"Stop," she commands, holding up her hand. "You can't do it. Not if you play fair. Not if you avoid dark magic. I may not know you, Kai, but I can tell you're the kind of person who leans toward good over evil. You seem like the decent sort, loyal to the right people. You wouldn't be here helping out a kingdom that isn't your own if you weren't. It's that goodness that will be your downfall, because Hammon is not good. He's the evilest son of a bitch to ever lead a pack. He's got this game weighted so heavily in his favor, there's no way you can beat him."

I study her for a moment before crossing my arms. "What aren't you saying?"

She glances away. "Remember when I told you he uses blood magic?"

"Yes."

She raises her eyes back to mine. "He didn't just figure out how to bind people to him. He delved into dark blood magic—the darkest. He fully corrupted his soul, so now he has unimaginable power. He's gone as dark as a shifter can, tying himself to the moon."

I stumble back a step. "You can't . . . You're saying that he . . ."

Eleni nods. "Yes. He's a werewolf."

I shake my head fervently, stumbling back another step. "No. That's a myth."

Eleni laughs bitterly. "If only it were a myth our lives would be so much easier. But it's not. It's dark blood magic that takes the natural, pure state of shifting and twists it to something unnatural and evil. It turns him into a beast on every full moon, the only night the blood oaths can be broken or transferred."

The hopelessness of the situation sinks around me. Even if she's exaggerating, even if she's holding something back, this isn't good. I don't know much about the myths surrounding werewolves, but I know they're not filled with good things. Their power is linked to the moon, allowing them to shift into beast-like creatures if they wish on the nights before and after a full moon. On the night of the moon, they don't have control over their shift, but they're practically invincible.

"That's why no one can beat him," Eleni continues, her voice weighted and quiet. "In order to free those under the blood oaths, Hammon has to be taken out on a full moon. And even then it's less about destroying the oaths and more transferring them to a new leader." She raises her eyes to mine and I can feel her loneliness. "There's no way."

Something in me twists and new determination rises. I still want to raise an army of shifters to help Astra, but now it's more. Hammon may not be the same vein of evil as Kato and the Dragkonians, but he's evil all the same. He's still a threat, and I'm going to take him down.

THREE

It's been almost four months since we lost Gaiya. Her murderer was sentenced and hung for his crimes, but it doesn't feel like enough. Not at times like this when I'm watching Leyana. She's with her closest friends. They're laughing and smiling, but her eyes are distant, unfocused. Every so often one of the other girls will address Leyana or cast a look her way and she'll force a tight smile and enter their conversion. Otherwise she's little more than a vacant shell.

"You look like a stalker."

I jump, startled by Nova's quiet approach. I shake it off and sigh, keeping my gaze fixed on Leyana.

"I'm worried about her."

Nova hums and steps to my side, crossing their arms. "She doesn't seem to have the same light she used to, does she?"

"She hasn't for far too long, and I'm not sure what to do about it."

"Maybe she needs a change of scenery."

I snap my attention to Nova. "What do you mean?"

Nova shrugs and meets my eyes. "I don't know. It can't be easy seeing the person you lost everywhere you look."

"You think we should leave the village?"

My words come out sharper than I intend and Nova raises their hands defensively.

"Look, I'm not saying you need to pack up and move away. You've both lived here your entire lives. This is your home. For some people, that's enough. But Leyana seems to be struggling here. Maybe if you went away for just a bit, allowed her some space to heal, it might help."

I swallow and look back at my sister. She's not even pretending to follow the conversation anymore. Nova is right; maybe a change is what we need. I run my hand through my hair and look away, letting my eyes take in the village I've called home for my entire life. As much as I want to help Leyana, I wouldn't even know where to begin. Unless . . .

"What?"

I scowl at Nova. "What do you mean 'What?'"

The corners of their lips twitch, threatening to turn into a smile. "You look like inspiration just struck. It was me, wasn't it? I gave you inspiration."

I scoff, though it sounds dangerously close to a laugh. Nova's grin breaks free and they bump their shoulder against mine.

"Come on. Admit it. I inspired you."

I shake my head, fighting back my own grin. "You . . . gave me something to think about." I cast one last look toward Leyana before turning away. "And now I'm leaving so I can go figure something out. If Leyana starts looking for me, let her know I went home."

"Sure thing!" they call after me.

I waste no time crossing through the village. I know exactly where the little journal is hidden—the one that's caused far too many problems—but maybe it's time for things to turn in my favor and the damn thing can be useful for once.

The journal isn't obviously important. In fact, I'm not convinced it holds any true significance to anyone outside my family, despite the way some people seem desperate to get their hands on it. It belonged to my great-grandfather. He received the journal for his sixteenth birthday and started recording immediately.

I crack the journal open and skim over the first several entries. It's relatively boring stuff, mostly accounts of everyday life. Then, a couple months in, he starts his research. He shares a story told to him by his uncle that deals with his—our—family history. According to legend, our family line can be traced back to the time when magic reigned and we were a family of powerful wolf shifters. My great-grandfather becomes obsessed with this fact and his next several entries are filled with ramblings, sketches, and theories. I pause on a page, taking in the intricate lines of a wolf, allowing my fingers to trace over its form.

I remember the first time I stumbled across this journal when I was a young boy. My mother pulled it from my hands and told me its contents were nonsense but, after much begging on my part, she caved and told me some of the stories within its pages. As a child I wanted to believe that a man could turn into a wolf and be as free as the journal claimed, but as I grew older and saw more of the world, those fantasies fell away. Now I want more than anything for them to be true.

I turn toward the back of the journal and find the entries detailing his trip to the Hundan Valley. I've heard rumors that magic dwells within those foreboding mountains—everyone has—but I don't believe it. The ink scattered across these pages tells a very different tale. It speaks of a home and freedom—something I long for. Visiting the Valley changed my great-grandfather's life.

I snap the journal shut. My great-grandfather didn't remain in the Valley, though he lived there for several years before word of his mother's illness drew him home. Several entries lament his departure and the pages hold less and less cheer, the last couple entirely empty. He came back to Aleahya, cared for his mother until she died, and married a sweet girl from Paravlia who came over the border with her merchant father. He lived a happy enough life, but he always longed to go back to the Valley.

The Valley changed him for the better, and I think it could be a breath of fresh air for us. Before I can doubt myself too much, I shove the journal in my pocket and head out of the house to find Nova. Even though they've never left our province, they're a bit of a cartographer, copying any and all maps they can find.

I find Nova not far from where I left them earlier, though they've been joined by a couple other town members. Nova pauses and turns toward me as I approach.

"Do you have a map I can borrow?" I ask without preamble.

Their face brightens. "A map, huh?"

"Yes," I say, my voice practically a growl. "A map."

"Hmm. It's possible." Their eyes twinkle mischievously. "I suppose you need it now?"

I glance at Nova's companions who are eyeing me warily and shake my head. "Not immediately, but soon would be nice. Whenever the time is convenient for you."

Nova studies me for a moment before turning back to the others. "I'll catch up with you all later. I think I need to help Kai with this."

The others give parting nods and wander off as Nova turns back to me. "Shall we go?"

"You didn't have to stop what you were doing."

Nova shrugs. "We weren't really doing much of anything. This clearly seems more important." Nova starts walking toward their house and I fall in step beside them. "Now, what kind of map did you need? Just Aleahya? Maybe a neighboring province? Or are you wanting to maybe tip into Paravlia?"

I glance away. "I need to map a path to the Hundan Valley."

Nova's eyes widen as they let out a low whistle. "The Hundan Valley? When I suggested you go somewhere else for a bit I thought you might go to neighboring village. Maybe head to the mountains. Check out the Paravlian border. I didn't think you were going to trek all the way across Gleador."

"I didn't really either but . . . well, I kind of have a familial connection there?"

Nova arches an eyebrow. "Familial connection? Are you sure? Because you don't sound sure."

We come to a stop outside their house and I sigh. "It's a long story, but suffice it to say that a relative of mine, long since passed, visited the Valley and it changed his life. He always intended to go back, to take his family, but it never happened. It was his dying wish."

"Dying wish? Did you even meet this relative?"

"Not exactly." I pull the journal out of my pocket and Nova's eyes widen.

"Is that . . . ?"

I nod, cutting them off. "It was my great-grandfather's. I don't know if the records in these pages are exactly true, or if they were his imagination and embellishments, but I'd like to find out. The fact that Leyana needs a change of scenery might just be the push I always needed to explore the possibility of its truth."

Nova nods. "I guess I can't begrudge you that." They grin. "So let's start by finding you a map!"

Nova ushers me inside, plucking up a pair of wire-rimmed spectacles so they can search through their papers to find what we need. Nova lays a map on the table, and we study it for a while, working together to figure out the best path to take. When I go to leave, Nova catches my wrist.

"Here," they say, rolling up the map and passing it to me. "Take this with you."

"Nova, I can't—"

They hold up their hand, silencing me. "You can and you will." They pause, offering me a smile that's sad around the edges. "That way you can not only find your way there, but also find your way back if and when you're ready."

Their words tug at something in my chest and I pull them into a tight hug before I can debate the motion. Nova's surprised huff blows the hair around my ears before I feel the low rumble of laughter in their chest as they return the embrace.

"And here I thought you were closed off to emotions."

I pull back and look into their shining eyes and manage a small grin. "I just hide them well. Thank you, Nova. This means . . . this means a lot."

"Just keep in touch, yeah?" Nova says, removing the spectacles sliding down their nose to fold them and slip them in their vest pocket.

I give them a sharp nod. "I will. I promise."

Before I can talk myself out of it, I rush home and begin preparations. I take into consideration the possible changes in weather and the trickiness of the terrain we'll have to cross on foot. I've figured out a reasonably solid plan when I'm pulled from my deep thoughts by Leyana's soft voice.

"Kai?"

I look up from the map into a pair of concerned dark eyes.

"What are you doing?"

I straighten from my hunched position and glance away. "I thought we might take a little trip."

"A trip?"

"Yes." I force my attention back to her. "To the Valley."

Her eyes widen. "The Valley? As in the Hundan Valley? On the opposite end of Gleador?" I nod. "Why?"

I study her face, trying to gauge her reaction as I say, "There are too many ghosts haunting us here. I thought maybe a place with fewer sad memories might give you—us—a chance to heal properly."

Her lips part and her brow furrows. "So you don't just mean a trip to the Valley for a visit. You mean for us to stay."

I lift a shoulder in a half-shrug. "If we find it fits."

Her gaze falls to where I've laid the journal on the table and recognition flickers across her face. She reaches for the journal and turns it tenderly over in her hands, carefully flipping through the pages in a way that could almost be considered affectionate.

"I always thought there might be truth to these records," she says, her voice barely above a whisper.

"You—you've read it?"

She lifts shining eyes to me and nods. "I have." Color rises in her cheeks and she looks away, almost ashamed. "I never told you or Gaiya because I thought if I did, if I shared my hope that it might be true, you would laugh at me." She sheepishly meets my eyes, dipping her head. "I wanted to hold to the dream that magic still exists somewhere in this world."

A smile tugs at my lips. "I like the idea, too."

She grins, passing the journal to me. "So, you think the stories are true, then?"

I shrug, accepting the journal and opening to a random page. "I have no idea, but like you, I want them to be."

"When do we leave?"

I sigh and set the journal down, turning my focus to the map. "Well, we have the winter months fast approaching. If we don't manage to leave within the next week or so, it would be best to wait until spring."

Her cheer falters and she nods.

"But," I say quickly, willing to bring the light back to my sister's eyes, "if we can make quick preparations, pack lightly, we could leave in a few days."

Everything about her brightens, as if a heavy burden has lifted from her shoulders.

"Let me know what we need, and I will help you prepare."

I step around the table between us and rest my hands on her shoulders. She turns her face up to mine.

"You are sure you don't mind leaving the only home you have ever known?"

She looks away, her eyes unfocused, but I know she sees what I often see—Gaiya's broken and twisted body.

"Like you said," she says, her voice so soft I hardly catch her words, "there are far too many ghosts here." Silence fills the air for a few ticks before she straightens her shoulders and forces a smile. "Besides, I think a magical adventure sounds a bit fun, don't you?"

A small chuckle escapes and I pull her into a half hug. "That I do, Leyana. That I do."

FOUR

It very quickly becomes evident that Eleni is by no means a morning person, but she is the one that insisted we wait to set out this morning. As much as I wanted to be on the road at first light, I knew she had been traveling for days and figured she could use the rest. Now that she and I are on our way, I wish I could have given in to her request to wait even later. Between the evil glances she keeps shooting over her shoulder and the snide remarks she makes every five minutes, I'm not entirely sure we will both make it to our destination alive.

According to Eleni, someone in a village a day-and-half to the east has more information about Hammon's operation. He recently recruited several young people from the village and a few of the elders took it upon themselves to retaliate. Most of them were lost in the battle, but the one who survived may be able to shed more light on Hammon's operation and confirm his current location.

We break midway through the day and eat from our rations of dried meat and fruit. Eleni doesn't speak much, but every time she looks my way, she scoffs and shakes her head. I ignore her and we get back on our way. The terrain is not easy. Lots of woods and uneven ground make for rough travel on a good day, but add in the snow, ice, and blistering winds and it's practically torture. The weather gets progressively worse throughout the day and Eleni is the first to cave and shift into her wolf form. I follow suit and we travel until it's even too dark to see with our wolf eyes.

I set up the tent—we only have one, unfortunately—while Eleni builds a fire. Once the flames stretch high, she pulls a tin cup and a small, bent bowl from her pack and begins adding something to it to heat over the fire. A warm, sweet scent fills the air and I find myself leaning toward it.

"Let me guess, you've never had hot chocolate before?" Eleni says with a grin that's borderline a sneer.

"If you're talking about that"—I nod to the concoction—"the answer is no."

Her grin turns more sincere as she digs out a second cup. "Well, Kai, prepare to have your life changed."

I watch, intrigued, as she pours a molten liquid from the bowl into the cups. I take mine hesitantly when it's offered and raise it to my nose to take a good sniff. It's heavenly. I sip it tentatively and my eyes widen. Eleni laughs.

"Told you." She takes a sip form her own cup and sighs, closing her eyes. "Nothing better."

As much as I want to disagree, I can't. We sit in silence while we enjoy our chocolate. When we finish, Eleni rises without saying word and heads into the tent. I give her a few minutes to prepare her bed before I join her. I settle on my own cot and am nearly asleep when her voice breaks the silence.

"You know this whole trip will likely be wasted."

I roll over and look toward where she's lying, though I can barely make out her form in the darkness.

"What?"

I hear more than see her turn over to face me.

"You're wasting your time."

I grit my teeth. "You've made your thoughts on that quite clear."

She sighs and turns back over. "You don't get it. I can see your determination, but you'll see. After we get to Bakra, you'll see how pointless this all is."

"I'm not turning back. I have people counting on me."

"Do these people even know what you're willing to risk for them?"

"It doesn't matter."

She sits up. "Doesn't it though? You're risking your life on a maybe. Nobody deserves that kind of devotion."

I prop myself up on my elbow. "Who betrayed you?"

She jerks so violently I can see it despite the darkness. "Nobody."

I push up into a sitting position. "Really? Because in my life experience when someone is as set against helping others as you are, it's because they were hurt in the past."

Eleni scoffs, shifting on her cot. "You want to know my story? Fine. No one betrayed me. They loved me. My mother loved me. My father loved me. And they loved each other so much it hurt. They were so damn happy. *We* were happy. But then my father died. His heart gave out. He left my mother and I, and my mother couldn't take it. She closed up into herself and couldn't do more than sit in a chair and stare out a window. I was was nine—*nine*—and I had to fend for myself. I had to watch my mother waste away to nothing and die slowly of a broken heart. For two damn years I had to put up with that. And, when her suffering was finally over, I was the one who buried her in the ground next to my father."

She falls silent and collapses back onto her cot, her back

to me. "So no one hurt me, not intentionally, but everyone will leave you eventually. The people you're here for, the people you want to help? They'll leave you one way or another."

She pauses and when she speaks again, her voice has lost its sharpness.

"You're like me, Kai. We're lone wolves. We don't need packs like other shifters might. We're better alone. I think when you see the empire Hammon is building, you'll realize I'm right. When you see the horrors he's committed and what he plans to do next, you'll leave. You'll decide it's not worth the fight."

I let her words sink in and I shake my head, although I know she can't see me. "I think you're wrong." She scoffs but I continue. "Because before I even arrived in the last *orta,* I had heard of your mission to take down Hammon. You care, Eleni, and you want justice to be served just like I do. I think that's why you're helping me. You're not a lone wolf. You don't really want to be alone."

"You're wrong."

"Maybe. Either way, I'm seeing this through." I lower onto my cot and adjust my blankets. "Now get some sleep. I'd like to make it to Bakra by noon tomorrow."

WE GET on the road early in the morning, neither of us wanting to prolong our journey any longer than necessary. We shift immediately, racing in our wolf forms. We make good time and arrive well before our goal of noon. Eleni speaks the dialect much better than I do and makes arrangements for us to meet with the man who can give us information on Hammon. Nerves swell in my gut when a young woman finally leads us to a low hut marked with black and silver mourning ribbons that twist angrily in the wind.

It takes a moment for my eyes to adjust to the dim lighting inside, but when they do my attention settles on the lone figure next to a flickering fire, a man well into his sixties. I startle, not expecting the deep gashes that mar his face or the milky, unseeing eyes beneath the scars.

"Thank you for taking the time to speak with us," Eleni says, her voice uncharacteristically gentle.

He nods and motions for us to take a seat across from him on the other side of the fire.

"I hear you are seeking information on Hammon?" he says, his voice rough and his accent thick and tripping over the Common dialect.

"If you have anything to share, it would be appreciated," I say, my own voice quiet.

Our host turns his attention to me and I shift awkwardly, unsettled by his visionless gaze.

"Where are you from?"

The question takes me off guard and my brain requires a moment to think of a reply. "I was born in Aleahya, but spent my recent years in the Hundan Valley. I'm here on a mission from Callenia."

"And your names?"

"My name is Eleni. I'm from the North, near Marnvi."

I clear my throat. "I'm Kai."

"Welcome, Eleni, Kai," he says, nodding to us each in turn. "My name is Jaknar and I will happily answer whatever questions I can. I fear it might not do much to further your endeavors, however."

"We will take whatever information you can share," I say quickly.

Jaknar nods. "Knowledge is power, indeed, but to defeat

someone as evil as Hammon, more power is needed than knowledge can provide. You will need wit and strength. Do you have those?"

"I believe I do."

"Good. And are you willing to risk your morals?"

"What?" I glance over at Eleni, but she refuses to meet my eyes, staring intently at Jaknar.

"I'm assuming you have a set of morals by which you live. I had one such set when I went against Hammon, and because I decided to stick to them, I failed." He gestures to his face. "By the time I realized that I would need to make significant changes to my intentions, it was too late. Too much was lost."

"You mean your sight?" Eleni asks, her voice hesitant.

Jaknar turns his attention to her. "My sight and my good looks are only part of what I lost. The cost was so much greater." He hangs his head, his expression sad. "And what I lost, I'm afraid can never be regained."

"If you're talking about whether or not I will kill Hammon, I have no reservations," I say, drawing his attention.

He nods. "That is good. But what about the blood oaths? Are you willing to take them on?"

I glance at Eleni before replying. "You mean the blood oaths sworn to Hammon?"

"Yes. If you truly defeat Hammon on his terms, the oaths sworn in blood to him will became your own to bear."

"I—I don't want that. I don't want anyone sworn to me."

Jaknar sighs. "I'm afraid you have no choice. Their burden will become your own, but that's not even the worst of it."

"What is worse than taking away the will of others?"

"Freely giving your own. The only way to beat Hammon is to swear a darker oath to the darkest magic."

I look over at Eleni and meet her eyes. Everything about

her stern gaze says "I told you so," but I refuse to give in. I shake my head firmly.

"No. There must be a way to defeat him without stooping to the depths he did."

"I can tell you that you are very wrong. I wish you weren't. I wish there were another way, but there is not. You cannot beat Hammon alone. You need the dark magic on your side."

I stand abruptly, hands clenched into fists at my side. "Darkness cannot beat darkness. Only light can chase it away."

Jaknar sighs. "I pray to the gods you can find a way to prove that, but my experience says otherwise. I do wish you luck."

"Thank you. Can you show us the way?"

He nods, the motion casting strange shadows across his scars. "I can." He raises his voice only slightly and calls out, "Arna, the map, if you please."

The woman who led us to the hut enters, casting a sharp glance our way before heading to the corner to shuffle through several papers. She pulls out a worn, yellowed map and hands it to Jacknar. He takes it in his wrinkled hands, tracing his fingers over the lines of ink. I wonder how he is able to tell the difference in the slight textures between ink and paper, until I notice the slight glow of his fingertips. Magic.

"Here," he says, tapping a spot on the map.

I move around the fire and sink next to him. He's pointing out a large village, perhaps even what might be deemed a city, to the northeast.

"That should only take two days."

Eleni's voice startles me. I'd been so lost in the map I hadn't realized she'd stepped behind me. I recover quickly and glance over my shoulder at her.

"Do you want to leave this afternoon?"

She shakes her head. "No. I've had enough travel for today. We can leave tomorrow, if you're still so determined to go."

I push up from the ground and face her, my body mere inches from hers. "You know I am."

Her eyes search mine for a moment as if she's trying to find the lie, the weakness. In the end, she must see my stubborn determination.

"So be it."

Without another word she sweeps from the hut. I'm tempted to follow her, but my manners hold me in my place. I swallow and look back to Jaknar.

"Thank you for your time." I shoot a glance at Arna, so she knows she's included in my thanks. "Your help is most appreciated."

Jaknar's face is somber as he replies, "I only wish I could have given you good news instead of sending you to your death."

I struggle to find the words to form a reply, but Arna steps froward before anything works its way out.

"Come with me. I will take you to a home that has agreed to host you for the night."

I nod and follow her for the hut. We walk quietly through the *orta*, several pairs of eyes following our trail. Arna stops outside another hut and motions me inside. I thank her and step through the doorway. I don't find my host for the evening, but I do find Eleni standing in the corner, arms crossed.

"You thought if you brought me to Jaknar that I would be swayed away."

"I hoped he might show you sense, yes."

"Did we even need to talk to him? Or did you know where Hammon was the entire time?"

She avoids my eyes, glancing away. "I wasn't sure if he was still in the same place. He tends to move." She lifts her gaze to me. "Either way, you needed to hear from someone else what a lost cause this all is."

"Your plan failed. I'm not backing down."

"My plan"—she takes a wide step closer—"was to make sure you really knew what you were getting into. See it with your own eyes. Now that you have?" She shrugs. "I'll lead you to your willing death."

I take a step closer to her. "And if I don't die?"

She makes a sound that could almost be confused for amusement. "Then, Kai, I will admit my misjudgments and help you lead your army home victorious."

FIVE

Leyana's gaze is fixed ahead, locked on the outline of the mountains against the burnt orange of the setting sun. After a little over two weeks of rough travel, I know she's ready to be done, but the look in her eyes is more than satisfaction at nearing the end of our journey. What I notice most is her hope.

"How much longer before we arrive?" she asks.

"We should reach the mountains tomorrow," I reply, shifting the pack on my shoulder. "I'm not sure how long it will take us to travel over them to get to the Valley itself, but I would assume it shouldn't take more than a handful of days."

She nods before turning her attention to me, a smile spreading across her face. "I can't wait to see if it's everything I imagined."

"Try not to be too disappointed if everything in the journal is fiction," I warn, resuming our previous pace, hoping to cover a little more distance before we stop for the night.

Leyana rolls her eyes. "I know. You've only told me a hundred times." She gives a little hop. "But even if I don't get to turn into a wolf, it's still a whole new chance at life. A way to start over."

"I know. I really hope everything works out for both of us there."

"Maybe you'll finally settle down with someone," she teases, bumping my arm with her shoulder.

A small huff escapes me. "I don't ever see that happening."

Leyana glances sideways at me. "You're really happy alone, aren't you?"

"I'm not alone. I have you. And you take a good bit of my focus."

She laughs, shaking her head. "It's not the same and you know it. Besides, what if I meet someone in the Valley and fall deeply and madly in love?"

"If the person is decent and kind and treats you well, then I wish you all the happiness."

She sighs dramatically. "That's not what I meant. What will you do without me to worry and fret over?"

"Ley, I will always worry about you as long as you live." I pause, shooting her a grin. "Even if you think you're technically someone else's problem."

"Hmm," Leyana muses, pretending to consider me for a moment. "I suppose I'll always be your problem, huh, Kai?"

I chuckle and pull her into a side hug. "You bet." I press a kiss to the top of her head. "Though you're not a problem, Ley."

She grins up at me. "Come on, Kai. I know I can be a little bit of a problem." A shadow crosses her face and she looks away. "After all, we wouldn't be traveling across the kingdom if it weren't for—"

"Hey," I cut her off. "None of that. We *both* needed a change of pace and location."

"Really? You're not just saying that?"

I give her a squeeze. "I'd never lie to you, Ley." I sigh and glance off. "To be honest, I'd been considering a change for a while. I've wondered about the truth behind the journal since I first discovered it."

"Well, onward, then!" she crows, pulling out from my arm and leaping ahead. "Onward to our destiny!"

I chuckle and pick up my pace.

As anticipated, we reach the mountains the next day. Travel over the rough terrain isn't easy, but we manage to keep a good pace. Thankfully, this small cluster of mountains isn't all that tall, so we reach the topmost area within a couple days. The mountaintop is filled with thick forests complete with towering trees and thick underbrush.

Leyana moves along silently, her curious eyes taking in our new surroundings with wide-eyed wonder. I'm watching her more than our surroundings, so we're both caught unaware by the guards.

"Who are you?" A sharp voice demands as a blade is pressed between my shoulder blades. "And what are you doing in our forest?"

I freeze as Leyana turns around, her normally bright eyes dimmed by terror. I slowly raise my hands in surrender, my pack dropping to the ground as another young man steps out from the trees near Leyana.

"We don't mean any trouble," I reply, working hard to keep my voice steady. "My sister and I are looking for the Hundan Valley."

"Why?" the man behind me demands, pressing his blade a little more firmly against my back.

"W-we had family in the Valley once," Leyana answers

before I do, her voice trembling. "We've come to explore our roots."

"Is that so?" the man closest to her asks, moving so he's less than a foot away. "Can you prove it?"

Leyana scowls and straightens her shoulders, raising her chin. "Maybe."

"Show us," the man behind me commands.

Leyana crosses her arms and glares at the man. "Why should I?"

The man near her blinks in shock, but the man behind me doesn't seem as surprised by her sudden bravery, pressing his blade so hard it cuts through my shirt, grazing my skin. I hiss and stumble forward. Leyana's eyes widen.

"Well, I have a sword at your brother's back that I could easily push through his heart. Perhaps you should take heed."

Leyana's fear fades into fury. Before I can register her movements, she has a small dagger drawn—I don't even know where she got it—and presses it against the neck of the man near her.

"And maybe you shouldn't threaten travelers simply looking for answers," Leyana hisses, twisting the blade under the man's chin so he's forced to lift his head to avoid being cut.

"Leyana," I say, my voice filled with warning.

Leyana looks at me and shakes her head. "What, Kai? I'm supposed to let them threaten you?"

"I assume they're doing their job," I offer, working hard to keep my breathing steady.

"Y-yeah. That's all," the man beneath Leyana's blade says. "It's our duty to watch the borders of the Valley."

"And that requires you to draw blades at every weary traveler that crosses your path?" Leyana asks, shaking her head. "Piss poor work if you ask me."

The man behind me chuckles and lowers his sword. I

quickly step away and spin to face him. He's younger than I thought, eighteen at the oldest. His eyes trail over me and he shakes his head before sheathing his sword and extending his hand.

"My name's Mahk."

I stare down at his hand for a moment before accepting, squeezing his hand harder than necessary. He winces but doesn't say anything. Leyana watches our interaction before cautiously lowering her dagger. The man she had at knife point stumbles back, running a hand over his neck.

"We really didn't mean any harm, but it is our job to guard the borders," Mahk says. "You can never be sure who might try to cross into the Valley."

I rake a hand through my hair and nod. "We understand."

"Do we though?" Leyana asks cocking an eyebrow. She turns to the man closest to her. "What is your name, anyway?"

"My name?" the man asks, blinking at Leyana. "Um, Kiaan. My name is Kiaan."

Leyana considers him for a moment before nodding, sliding her dagger into her sleeve where I assume she has some sort of hidden sheath. "I've heard worse names."

Kiaan nods, blushing. Mahk rolls his eyes.

"So, are we allowed into the Valley?" I ask, turning my attention to Mahk.

He frowns. "Well, we are supposed to keep out threats."

"We're no threat!" Leyana insists.

"Tell that to Kiaan," Mahk mutters.

Leyana puts her hands on her hips. "I wouldn't have actually cut him. Besides, you had a sword at my brother's back. Was I just supposed to let you kill him?"

Mahk's eyes widen. "I wasn't going to *kill* him! I don't kill people!"

"Right. You just threaten innocent travelers."

I sigh and lean down to grab my pack. Leyana and Mahk continue arguing as I dig through the contents and pull out the journal. I flip it open and find the page I need, thrusting it in Mahk's face.

"Like you would do any— Hey! What's this?" He accepts the journal and blinks down at the open page for a moment before lifting his eyes to me. "This is why you're here?"

I nod. "Is that enough to be allowed in?"

Mahk's eyes scan the page again for a moment before he snaps the journal shut. "It should be enough. If nothing else, Follik will likely want to meet you."

Mahk hands the journal back and I slip it into my pocket instead of my pack.

"Come on," Mahk instructs, taking a step forward and waving for us to follow him.

Leyana and I obediently fall in line behind him, Kiaan taking up the rear. We only go a few yards before an unfamiliar feeling tickles across my skin. With each step the feeling grows and I glance over my shoulder at Leyana, whose face practically glows. A small giggle escapes and I know she can feel the same sweet warmth in the air I can. Kiaan watches her, his own eyes shining.

"It's the magic," he whispers, mostly to Leyana but I catch his words as well.

Leyana looks back at him. "So it's real? The stories are real?" Kiaan nods and Leyana looks back to me, eyes brighter than I've ever seen them. "Kai! The journal is real!"

"Don't get too excited," Mahk cuts in, keeping his attention fixed on the path ahead. "Just because you can feel the magic doesn't necessarily mean you can use it, even if sensing it may be a good sign." He glances back at us. "You'll understand more after you talk to Follik."

We weave between the trees, Mahk leading us to a cliff

overlooking the Valley below. Leyana gasps, stepping danger-ously close to the edge. I resist the urge to reach out and pull her back, trusting her enough to keep her own balance.

"It's beautiful," she whispers, awe filling her voice.

Mahk's eyes shine with pride as he nods. "It is." He looks over his shoulder to Kiaan. "Help me wisp them down and then we can come back up and finish our rounds."

Kiaan nods sharply, clearly understanding the order, but I frown.

"What do you mean by 'wisp'? What is that?"

Mahk grins, holding out his hand. "Give me your hand and find out."

I exchange a wary glance with Leyana, who shrugs. With a heavy sigh, I shift the pack on my shoulder and follow Mahk's order. His grin grows and suddenly the ground beneath my feet vanishes. I feel light and heavy all at once, the world spin-ning around me and taking new shape. I gasp and stumble back as my feet hit the ground. Mahk grins at me as Kiaan appears a few feet away with Leyana in tow. She looks just as breathless as I feel.

I blink and look around. We're no longer on a cliff looking down into the Valley itself. No, we're *in* the Valley on one of the bridge pathways built against the mountainside.

"That was wisping," Mahk says, his eyes shining with mischief. "If you truly have magic, you can learn to do it on your own next. Now, follow me. I'll take you to Follik."

Leyana falls into step next to me and whispers, "That was amazing!"

I nod, my stomach still swooping from the wisping. It was amazing. If that little taste of magic can make me feel this way, I can only imagine what the full brunt of magic can do.

It takes a few minutes for everything to get sorted and everyone important to be found, but as soon as everything is arranged, Leyana and I find ourselves in a meeting room of sorts before a tall man with bronze skin and jet-black hair who I assume is Follik. At his side are two teens: a boy that can't be much more than fifteen who looks like a younger version of Follik himself and a young girl around twelve or thirteen with tan skin and brown hair twisted in several braids.

"Let's make this quick," the man says, taking a seat at the table. "Dinner is starting and I'm hungry."

The two teens glare at each other but remain standing. The man looks up at me, aggravation lining his features. I quickly take a seat to his right and Leyana sits in the chair next to me.

"I understand you're claiming you had family in the Valley at some point?"

I nod, pulling the journal from my pocket and sliding it across the table to Follik. He opens it, flipping through, pausing occasionally to study a page. The teens peer over his shoulder. After a few minutes he snaps the journal shut and hands it back.

"That looks legitimate enough. Did you feel magic when you entered our borders?"

"Yes, sir," I reply with a nod. I glance at Leyana. "We both did."

The man exhales through his nose and shrugs. "We're not prone to turning away those with claim to our Valley."

"But, father," the teenage boy speaks up. "Shouldn't we make extra sure?"

Follik glances over his shoulder at his son. "What do you suggest, Deven?"

The boy straightens under his father's gaze. "I say we check our records and make sure that their relative was in good standing in the Valley."

Follik nods approvingly. "That is a good suggestion." He

turns his head to look at the girl who is glaring daggers at the boy. "And you, Jessalynn? What do you suggest?"

The girl turns her glare to me, crossing her arms. "Even if we find evidence that their relative was in good standing, they need to prove their worth."

Follik raises an eyebrow. "Oh? How so?"

"The Valley doesn't need any more dead weight. If they stay, they work. They train to hone their magic."

Deven snorts, shaking his head. Jessalynn's attention snaps to him. "What?"

Deven rolls his eyes. "You can't just force people into work detail," he drawls. "And what if they don't have magic?"

"They just said they did!"

"No, they said they felt the magic. There's a difference, little Jess. And people think you'll be able to lead one day."

"I—"

"Enough!" Follik cuts them off. "You're both correct." He turns his attention back to me and Leyana. "We will confirm that your family is in good standing. If it is, we will expect you to play your part in the operation of the Valley. We work together here to keep things running. If you don't have accessible magic, we will not make you leave." He sends a sharp look at the teens behind him before looking back to us. "If you do, however, we will help you train and learn to use your magic."

Follik pushes up from his chair and offers me a sharp smile. "For the time being, you will be our guests. As long as you don't threaten my people or disrupt the flow of work, you are welcome to stay while we look into your family's history. We'll find a volunteer to host you later, but for now, let's go get some dinner."

Leyana and I exchange a look as we rise and follow Follik from the room. Somehow it feels like we're home, or something very close to it.

SIX

Eleni and I stay in our wolf forms most of the time to help against the biting wind and snow. We only shift into our human forms if we set up camp or when we need to build a fire or eat. It's already nearing night when we approach our destination. Even from this distance I can tell it's much larger than any of the *ortas* I've visited and is much closer to the large city the queen brought me to when we first entered Paravlia.

We're still a few miles out when Eleni stops, shifting. I join her, stepping to her side, but she keeps her gaze fixed on the gated city ahead.

"This is as far as I can go."

I frown. "What do you mean?"

She looks over at me, her eyes cold. "You asked me to bring you to Hammon. Well"—she nods to the city—"there he is."

"That's just the city where he may possibly be. That doesn't mean he's actually there."

"He's definitely there."

"How can you . . ." I trail off as realization strikes. "You've sworn a blood oath."

She clenches her teeth. "I assure you I didn't have a choice."

"Damn it, Eleni!" I yell, throwing my hands in the air. "This is key information that might have been good to know ahead of time."

"I'm telling you now. That's all that matters."

I continue glaring and she sighs. "Look, I filled my end of the deal. I never promised you I would fight or help you beyond bringing you here. I played my hand before and lost. I was lucky to get far enough from his pull, and I'm not stupid enough to go back in. I'm a lone wolf, and I'm fine with that." She considers me a moment before adding, "As a lone wolf yourself, surely you get what I'm saying."

I grind my teeth. As much as I hate to admit it, she's right. I'm good at doing things on my own.

"Fine. I assume you'll go back home?"

She shrugs. "Where's home anymore? Maybe I'll stick around, just in case you pull off a miracle."

"I thought you said I was as good as dead."

She grins. "I said I think you're going to die, doesn't mean I hope you will." She sobers, glancing back toward the city. "In fact I hope you give the bastard a taste of his own medicine and take him down."

I take a deep breath and release it slowly. "Yeah, I hope so, too." I look down at her. "So I guess this is goodbye?"

"Perhaps. If you make it out alive, I'm sure I'll see you again. After all, my oath and loyalty will transfer to you."

"And if I don't?"

"I'll throw a rose on your grave."

She turns and starts to walk away. After a few steps, she turns and looks at me over her shoulder.

"*Ulvwara gotsënde*," she says, the accented words rolling over her tongue.

"What does that mean?"

"There's no direct translation, but essentially, it means 'may the gods' blessings give you luck.'"

I arch an eyebrow. "That's a long translation for such a short phrase."

"What can I say? We're efficient."

Without another word, she shifts into a wolf and bounds off. With a sigh, I bolster my strength and march toward the city. It doesn't take long before I reach the gates. A guard stands outside, eyeing me as I approach. When I stop in front of him, he speaks rapidly in a dialect I don't know. I shake my head and he calls out, banging his fist on the door behind him. A panel shifts and a face appears over his shoulder. The guard speaks quickly to the newcomer who eyes me warily.

"Who are you?" he asks in heavily accented Common. "And what is your purpose?"

"I've come seeking Hammon."

The guard snorts a laugh. "Who isn't? I take it you're a shifter?"

"Yes. A wolf."

"Oh, he'll like that."

"Until I take him down."

This time the man's laugh is full bellied. "Oh, sweet ignorance."

His next words in the other dialect must be a translation for the other man because they both laugh, shaking their heads at me. After a moment the lock disengages with a loud click and the gate swings open. I didn't expect to be let in after openly admitting to wanting to kill their leader, but I don't hesitate to walk through. The man I was speaking to steps out in front of me.

"You know you are likely walking to your death?"

A smile curls on my lips. "Maybe I'm walking to his."

The man gives me a pitying look. "Everyone thinks that until their body is burned to ash."

"You burn the bodies?"

The man frowns. "Of course. Even those foolish enough to go against Hammon deserve to have their ashes carried to the gods. Besides, the ground is too frozen right now to bury that many bodies."

I glance past the man into the bustle of the city. "And where might I find him?"

The man nods down the road. "You'll likely find him in Havran Hall."

"Havran Hall?"

"*Ja.* It's a gambling den of sorts, but where he does a good bit of his business. If he's not there, someone else can direct you elsewhere." He pauses before adding, "Good luck."

I give the man a parting nod and head into the city. At first, it's not much different than any other city I've visited, but as I reach the inner city I realize it's far more chaotic. Many of the citizens stumble through the streets, hoods pulled over their heads and bodies hunched to avoid detection. Meanwhile, other more . . . rambunctious people seem to have no issues doing whatever the hell they want. The closer I get to Havran Hall, the worse it all becomes. There's a clear power dynamic here, and it leaves a bitter taste on my tongue.

If I thought the streets were chaotic, they don't hold a candle to the inside of Havran Hall. From the moment I enter, something crawls across my skin in a very unsettling way, and every instinct I have tells me to run. I swallow hard and force my way through the crowd to what is obviously the main table. For one, it's set apart from the rest of the chaos, slightly raised on a platform. For another, no matter how involved the others are in their own games and debauchery, they keep casting glances toward the table, as if seeking out some sort of approval.

When I'm within a couple yards of the main table, a pair of guards—at least I assume they're guards based on their stance, wide build, and heavy scowls—block my way.

"Pardon me," I say in my most polite voice. "I need to speak with Hammon."

"No one just marches up to him," one of the guards snarls.

"What do you need with him, anyway?" the other asks.

I straighten to my full height, pleased to discover I have a couple inches on each of the men. "I've come to issue a challenge."

One man grins at me with a wide, toothy smile that's anything but friendly while the other outright laughs.

"Hey, boss!" the grinning one calls over his shoulder. "You've got a challenger."

"Oh, do I?" A smooth, deep voice calls back. "Well, by all means, let them in."

The guards part and for the first time I get a good glimpse of the table. There are ten people seated with a few more standing around the edges of the platform. The man at the head of the table stands slowly while the others snicker in clear amusement as they take me in. I allow myself a moment to size up my opponent, and, while I'm not entirely sure what I was expecting, this man doesn't align with my previous assumptions. He's tall with broad shoulders and a well-muscled figure, but he doesn't look like the kind of man I would expect to start a rebellion. No, the man standing staring down at me with interest gleaming in his eyes wouldn't look a bit out of place at a formal royal event.

"You've come to challenge me?" he asks, an amused smile twitching on his lips.

"Yes," I reply, clenching my hands in fists at my side.

"Hmm," the man muses, his eyes raking over me. "I've had more pathetic opponents. Tell me, what is your name?"

"Kai."

"All right Kai, and why have you come? What is your motivation?" I open my mouth to reply but he waves me off. "And I don't want the standard mush people often feed me about justice and the like. I want to know why you personally are taking this risk."

I swallow hard, debating how much truth I want to share.

"I was sent by your queen."

Hammon's eyes widen a fraction in surprise before he releases a full-bodied laugh that draws the attention of everyone in the room that isn't already looking our way. The cacophony behind me fades into an eerie silence.

"I have no queen."

I shrug. "She seems to disagree."

Anger flashes in his eyes. "And where did the queen dig you up from? You're not from here. How far did she have to hunt to find a 'worthy' champion for her lost cause?"

"That answer is a bit complicated."

"It always is. Give it a shot."

I take a steadying breath. "I'm from the Hundan Valley in Gleador, but the queen found me in Callenia, serving King Ehren and his Court Sorceress."

This doesn't seem to be the answer anyone was expecting. Hammon's eyebrows shoot up while murmurs fill the room in a heated buzz.

"Callenia? From what I've heard of the chaos and rebellion happening in Callenia, it surprises me to discover that they have people to outsource for a lost cause."

"If it were a lost cause, perhaps, but I don't believe it is."

Hammon snorts. "You really believe that? Fine. Fine! You

want to challenge me, then so be it. I accept. Of course, we have to wait for the full moon which is three days away. Until then"—he snaps his fingers and the guards move in, grabbing my arms—"we'll take care of your accommodations."

I struggle under the grip of my captors, but their hold is far too strong for me to fight off. Not that I necessarily would. If I'm going to go up against Hammon, I'm going to need to play the game by his rules.

"Nova, show our guest to his new quarters."

I still as soon as the words leave Hammon's mouth and my attention snaps to the figure moving away from those standing behind Hammon. The person that steps forward is older than I remember, but their features are familiar, though their once joy-filled eyes have gone cold. I barely dare to breathe as they cross the platform and step down, pausing mere inches away to stare into my eyes.

"Follow me," they say, turning away abruptly and weaving through the crowd.

My guards tighten their grip as I'm jerked along behind Nova. My instincts yell at me to fight and run, but I can't. I need to see this through, so I allow myself to be dragged out a back entrance and into a gutter ally. When we enter another building, I'm surprised to find it not very prison-like. I'm even more surprised when we stop in front of a sparse room with no door instead of a cell with bars.

"In you go," one of my guards growls, shoving me forward as the other yanks the pack from my shoulder.

I stumble but manage to stay upright. I turn and glare at my captors. The guards grin as they take a step back, Nova stepping forward. Nova raises their hands and a soft, red magic emanates from their palms. Soon the entire doorway is filled with the translucent light. I reach out and touch the magic tentatively. Even though I instantly jerk my hand back as the sharp magic bites and burns my skin, I can tell the barrier is as firm and solid as any door would be.

"You won't be able to escape," one of the guards says with a chuckle. "So don't even try."

Nova turns their head, giving their companions a cold look. "You may return to Hammon. I will make sure the prisoner is secure."

"But we're—"

"Go."

Both men look disgruntled at the demand but obey nonetheless, slinking down the hall. Once they're gone, Nova turns their attention to me.

"They're correct, you know. You won't be able to escape."

"I don't want to escape."

Nova scoffs. "Then you want to die."

"I want to free the people he has trapped. Why are you helping him, Nova? This isn't you."

Nova's face hardens, their eyes flashing. "You don't know me anymore, Kai. You don't know what is or isn't me."

"Well, it's not the Nova I knew."

"No," they spit. "The Nova you knew disappeared after they were abandoned." They take a step closer so they're practically pressed against their magical barrier. "The Nova you knew is long gone."

Their expression is so foreign, I wonder for a moment if the Nova I knew and cherished is even still in there. I wonder if this is how Astra feels, knowing that her brother, her twin, is no longer quite in control of himself. It's painful to have someone you love so close but trapped inside a version of themselves that you can't recognize.

"Why?"

It's the only thing I can manage, the only words I can form. Nova scowls.

"Why what?"

"Why are you on Hammon's side? Why are you so changed?"

"Maybe it's because best friend, one of the people I cared most about, left me."

My shoulders drop. I long to reach out and pull Nova closer, but I can't.

"Nova, I had to go. You know that."

Nova shakes their head, glancing to the side. "Right. For Leyana." They look back at me, their expression even more intense than before. "But you made it sound like you'd return at some point. You promised to stay in contact."

"I did."

Nova laughs, but it's bitter and humorless. "Three times you wrote me. Once from the road to let me know my map was accurate and once when you arrived to let me know you made it there safely. Then I didn't hear a word from you for *two years*, and that was just to let me know Leyana . . . that Leyana died. I wrote you dozens of times, desperate to keep my friend, but you never responded. I didn't know if you were dead or alive or what."

"I—I couldn't. There were restrictions on what I could share with you."

"You couldn't have told me anything about your lives? Not one thing? Not what you had for breakfast or whether you had a good night's sleep?"

Their expression is so hurt, I wonder what I could've done to keep them informed, what I could've done differently.

"Nova, I—"

"No. Just stop. It's too late for excuses now, Kai. You've made it pretty clear that you meant more to me than I ever meant to you. Otherwise, at the very least, you would've reached out once magic returned. Surely, you weren't beholden to keep your secrets even then?"

My mouth is suddenly dry. "Is that why you went to Hammon?"

Nova's face falls. "I didn't understand what was happening to me. I was the only one in Nara that seemed to have these new powers. My magic can be deadly. I was hurting people, people I loved. When I heard that there was someone willing to help those with magic not too far away in Paravlia, I followed the rumors."

"But surely, once you realized that Hammon wasn't a good man—"

"Who are you to judge who is a good man and who isn't?" Nova demands, their voice cold. "I found someone willing to help me, and I'm stronger now. I'm in his trusted circle."

"But at what cost?" I ask, my voice soft.

Something flickers in Nova's eyes. "I paid the price I felt I needed."

"Nova, you are worth so much more."

Nova straightens, pushing all emotions behind a carefully constructed mask.

"The past is the past. There's no point in focusing on what could've been." They start to walk away but pause after a few steps, their back still turned. "For what it's worth, I will mourn your death when Hammon kills you."

Without another word, they disappear.

SEVEN

Leyana and I are allowed the first few days to acclimate to the Valley while they check their records. Eyes follow us everywhere the first day or two, but once we are no longer perceived to be an active threat, people let us go about our day with less scrutiny. I'm starting to wonder if we've been forgotten in the day-to-day hustle, but after about a week we're summoned back before Follik. This time we're called directly to his office. He's seated behind his desk, and once again, Jessalynn and Deven stand behind him.

"Well, I have some good news," he says, not bothering to look up from the papers he's sorting on his desk. "We've confirmed your heritage and your family history is clean."

"So we can stay?" Leyana asks, her eyes bright.

Follik glances up, offering her a practiced smile. "Indeed. Of course"—he goes back to his papers—"you'll need to pull your weight, and in exchange we'll make sure you have housing and food and anything else you require. It's how the Valley runs."

"Do you have specifics in mind?" I ask, my aggravation at his inattention barely masked.

Follik doesn't answer right away, his eyes narrowed in on a page. "Here it is." He looks up from the page with a grin. "We have gaps in our food service, our quarry handlers, and our"—he squints at the page—"library sorting."

"Do we get to pick?" I ask.

Follik shrugs. "We like to match people with the places they feel the most comfortable and where their skillset will be the most useful. I assume you both have shifting magic like your grandfather?"

Leyana and I exchange a glance.

"We don't know," I confess.

Follik raises an eyebrow. "You mean you've been here a week and you haven't tried to access your magic? Can you even feel it?"

"We can feel the magic in the Valley, but we have yet to harness it."

"Well then," Follik muses, leaning back in his chair as he studies us, "we will have to remedy that. We have several excellent instructors you can work with to help you unlock your magic. Of course, you do understand that from this point on, everything you learn about magic will have to be kept secret from the world."

"Why?" Leyana asks.

Follik frowns. "If the world knew the magic we held, it could be catastrophic. We would either be swarmed with people seeking magical powers with no way to control or train them properly, or we would be attacked by people who fear our magic. Neither option is good. Therefore, secrecy is key to preserving life as we know it. If you find this to be difficult, there are measures we could take to erase the knowledge of its existence from your minds."

Leyana's eyes widen with something close to horror. "You have ways to erase our memories?"

Follik nods. "Indeed. We have potions crafted from magical minerals mined in the Valley that can do marvelous things. I assure you that if you choose that option, you will not be harmed, but they work more efficiently with less side effects the earlier they are administered. So, if you desire to leave the Valley your decision should be made soon."

I step forward, placing my body protectively in front of Leyana. "Are all your citizens made to forget if they choose to leave?"

"Those who have proven they can be trusted may leave at any time, but new residents, such as yourselves, have not yet proven your trustworthiness."

Even if I don't particularly like the idea of my memory being altered, I can understand the reasoning behind it.

"We can be trusted," I confirm with a nod. "We won't breathe a word of what we learn here to anyone."

"Good. Now that's established, shall we find you a job?"

I lick my lips. "What were the options again?"

Follik glances down at the paper. "Food service for the morning or evening meal, a runner or handler for the quarry, and record sorting in the library." He scowls, turning his attention to Leyana. "How old are you, dear?"

Leyana straightens. "Sixteen."

Follik nods thoughtfully. "Most of our citizens start working around the age of fifteen but we do not require it until you are eighteen."

Leyana lifts her chin. "I can do my part."

Follik chuckles. "Your choice. I think you may be well suited for the quarry. The job wouldn't be difficult and there's possibility for promotion if you do well. It gives you room to grow."

"That will work," Leyana says with a nod.

Follik turns his attention to me. "And you?"

"Food service would be fine."

"Very well." Follik makes a note on his paper. "Now, on to your living quarters. We have a few one-bedroom homes available, or there's a recently vacated two-bedroom."

"I think the two-bedroom if possible," I reply, glancing at Leyana who gives me an agreeing nod.

Follik makes another note. "Excellent. I will pass that information on and you will be contacted shortly with your job details. Deven, will you take these to Master Gerand and Mistress Carna respectively?"

Deven steps forward from where he's been watching silently, accepting the slips of paper from Follik. "Of course."

He leaves, casting us one last glance over his shoulder before he disappears out the door. Follik turns his attention to Jessalynn.

"And Jess, will you take our newest citizens to their residence?" He pulls another slip of paper from the stack on his desk and hands it to the girl. "And maybe explain to them about magic on the way? As a newer addition yourself, you are in a unique position to share your knowledge."

She steps forward with a nod. "Of course." She accepts the paper and lets her eyes trail over the writing.

"Do you know where to take them?"

Jessalynn nods.

"Excellent." Follik looks back to me. "Jess will take you to your new home and those in charge of your work positions will be in touch by the end of the day."

Jess makes brief eye contact before brushing past us. "Try to keep up."

We fall into step behind her, stepping out of the office onto one of the suspended bridges that cling to the side of mountain.

"What do you know about magic?" she asks as we walk.

"Not much, to be honest," I reply. "From what I've read in my great-grandfather's journal, I know it's somewhat innate."

Jess nods as if this is the answer she expected. "It is. It's something that's inside of you. You simply need to home in on it. Find where the magic lives. Once you find the source, you just have to pull it forward."

"How?" Leyana asks.

Jess glances over her shoulder with a scowl. "You just . . . do. I can't really explain that part. Once you try, you'll under-stand. It's like an energy of sorts."

She continues talking, trying her best to describe the sensation, Leyana hanging on her every word. I, instead, focus on finding the energy inside me that she's speaking of. I'm startled to discover how easy it is to find and identify. I don't dare pull on it here, however. It feels too risky to try, too intimate.

After a few minutes we come to an abrupt stop in front of what will be our new home. Jessalynn leaves us to explore. It's small, but more than big enough for the two of us. Leyana claims the room on the left, so I take the one on the right. Once we've gotten the layout down, we head to the home where we've been staying and fetch our things. It doesn't take long for us to get settled. When I exit my room, I find Leyana standing in the center of the main area, looking around glassy-eyed.

"You okay, Ley?" I ask, approaching her slowly and slipping my arm around her shoulders.

She leans into me, resting her head against my chest. "Yeah. I think it's just really sinking in that this is our new home."

"You know, if you're not comfortable here, we can leave. We don't have to stay."

She shakes her head. "No, I'm fine. I like it here. It's just . . . different."

"I understand that. Know, though, that if that ever changes, I will take you away from here."

"I know, Kai." She slips her arms around me and gives me a quick hug before she pulls back, her eyes shining. "Should we try our magic?"

I can't hold back my grin. "We could, but if we are shifters, maybe we should try shifting outdoors?"

Leyana laughs. "Yeah, maybe."

We leave together and make our way up one of the paths that leads to the wooded area overlooking the valley. It's not an extremely difficult hike, but I look forward to the day I can access my magic to wisp like many of the other residents. We find a nice clearing and stand facing each other.

"Okay," Leyana says, her forehead knitted in concentration. "Can you feel your magic? I think I can feel mine."

I nod. "I think I can feel mine as well."

"So I find it and pull it and . . . nothing." She sighs.

Her defeat only lasts for a moment before she's trying again. And again. And again.

"This is impossible!" she yells, throwing her hands in the air.

"It may take time, Ley, but you'll get it."

"*You* try it then," she demands, crossing her arms. "Maybe if you can do it, you can guide me."

"Okay," I say, my stomach suddenly swelling with nerves. "Stand back."

I take a deep breath and focus on the warmth of magic I found earlier. I reach into it and let it course over me. I don't try to force it. I merely ask, and the next thing I know, there's a strange coolness sweeping over me. The world twists and reshapes as I'm pulled into the magic. It prickles across my skin in a way that's a little uncomfortable, but it doesn't really hurt. It's only when Leyana gasps and I find myself looking up at her that I realize I've shifted.

"You did it! You did it, Kai!" Leyana says, bouncing up and down. "You're a wolf!"

I find the magic again and tug it, transforming back into a human. I'm relieved to find my clothes have remained intact.

"How?" she breathes.

"Don't force it. Let it work on its own."

She licks her lips, nodding. "Okay. I can do this."

She breathes in and closes her eyes. A moment later, I see the magic at work. It's different viewing it from the outside after experiencing it firsthand. It's beautiful. Leyana transforms into a thin, silver-gray wolf with sharp blue-gray eyes. Once she realizes her magic works, she gives a delighted yip. I laugh and pull on my own magic, shifting again. It takes a little more of my energy, but I don't mind. I have no intention of shifting back any time soon. My wolf half has been hidden away for twenty years. It deserves some time to be free.

Together Leyana and I race through the trees, freer than we have ever been before.

EIGHT

No one visits me in captivity, except to bring scant amounts of food that taste strangely bitter, and I regret not having the forethought to keep some food on my person. The first night, everything remains quiet, but the second I can hear the howls of the beasts as they roam. Everything about the sound is unnatural, sending chills across my spine and twisting my stomach into knots. My nature recognizes the wrongness and I shift to ease my inner wolf. I pace back and forth, ready to fight off any attack. A sound echoes down the hall and I go on alert, my eyes trained on the doorway. I relax only slightly when a familiar face appears.

"Look at you wolfing out," Eleni teases, her hands on her hips.

I shift into my human form and take a step closer to the doorway. "What are you doing here? I thought you made a run for it."

She grins. "Yeah, I thought I was going to run, too, but something tells me to stick around this time."

"I thought you were concerned about Hammon taking you again."

She shrugs, but I can see the worry in her eyes. "He's preoccupied and on the hunt tonight. He's not paying attention to his home base, making it the perfect time to come check on you. Has your food tasted funny?"

I frown. "A bit."

She sighs, digging into the bag at her side. "I figured as much. They have a tendency to taint the food with a potion that will make your magic weaker. Luckily, I have a cure."

She pulls a small vial from the bag and frowns at the magic blocking the doorway.

"Of course, it won't help if I can't get it to you." She reaches out to touch the magic and jerks back with a hiss. "Shit! That hurts!"

She steps back, her brows knit in concentration as she studies the buzzing magic.

"There must be some way around it," she mutters, moving around to examine it from different angles.

"You won't be able to get through." Nova's voice floats down the hall.

Eleni spins and faces the direction Nova is coming from. She tenses, ready for an attack, but she only takes a step back as Nova steps into view, their hands in their pockets.

"Is this your magic?" Eleni demands, nodding to the doorway.

Nova takes her in before nodding. "It is, and it is very strong. It not only keeps him in and you out, but it alerts me when an unwanted presence is near." They turn to me. "How are you faring?"

"Well, I just learned that what little food I've been given is poisoned to make sure I lose, so I'm not doing too great right now."

Nova winces. "Ah, yes. Hammon tends to do that with anyone he actually thinks might have a chance. That means you definitely made an impression."

"Bravo for me. I'd prefer for him not to cheat any more than he already is. Are you here to gloat?"

Nova glances away. "No, I—" They look up and meet my eyes. I can practically feel their guilt. "Your presence took me off guard. I think, perhaps, I did not react the best that I could. Though, given my circumstances, there wasn't much I could do. Hammon has eyes everywhere."

"Wait," Eleni cuts in, taking a step closer. "Do you two know each other?"

Nova nods sheepishly as I answer. "We basically grew up together."

She glares at Nova. "And yet you're willing to lead him to his death?"

Nova raises their hands. "I never said that! I would rather Kai live. In fact," they say, turning their attention to me, "I talked to Hammon and he agreed that instead of killing you outright, he'll give you the option to take the blood oath and join him as one of his werewolves."

"What? I would never do that!" I yell, marching forward so the only thing separating me from Nova is their magical barrier. "What makes you think I would?"

Nova swallows hard and whispers, "I don't want you to die, Kai."

"Well, then give him this," Eleni says, holding up the vial and giving it a little shake.

Nova frowns and takes the vial from her. They hold it eye level, squinting at the contents. "What is it?"

"It's a potion that will counteract the poison your boss has been feeding him. It will also allow him to heal a little faster. If you want Kai to have a fighting chance, he needs that potion."

Nova swallows again, glancing nervously between me and Eleni. After a moment they nod.

"Fine." They turn to me. "I can't take down the whole barrier. Someone will sense it. But I can slip this through without anyone detecting the shift in magic."

I nod and Nova slowly reaches forward, manipulating a small hole in their magic and slipping the vial through. As soon as my fingers touch the coolness of the bottle, the barrier snaps closed.

"Wait to drink until right before you're taken to the fight," Eleni instructs as I turn the vial over in my hands. "It will have the strongest effect that way."

A door closes somewhere in the building and Nova and Eleni both jump.

"I need to go," Nova says, glancing around nervously. They nod at Eleni. "And you should, too."

Eleni nods. "I've already been here longer than I intended. Good luck, Kai. I really hope you win."

A moment later, she's gone. Nova turns to me.

"Look, Kai, I'm sorry about the things I said yesterday. I don't blame you for my choices. I missed you so much after you left, but a part of me knew you'd never return."

I manage a small smile. "I missed you, too, Nova."

They return my smile, but it fades quickly. "Look, Kai, even with whatever is in that potion, you don't have a chance against Hammon—not in his beast form. If you're given the chance to live, take it."

I shake my head firmly. "I can't, Nova. I would rather die than be forced to become one of his blood-bound beasts."

Nova clenches their teeth. "Don't be foolish, Kai."

"And don't you expect me to go against everything I stand for."

Footsteps echo nearby and Nova takes a step back. "Whatever. Just let it be known that I tried to help. Your death is on you now."

And with that, they disappear.

~

THE NEXT DAY I'm fed more meals, each laced with even more of the poison that's meant to take my energy. I eat only enough of the food so I don't feel hungry, leaving most of it on the plate. When night starts to fall, I drink the potion Eleni gave me. It's extremely bitter, making me gag, but I down it in one shot. Not much later, Nova appears with four guards to escort me to the battle.

I'm dragged unceremoniously through the streets to the middle of the city where a crowd has gathered. They part, jeering at me as I'm steered toward the center where a battle ring has been created, the edges of it marked with a buzzing gray magic that seems similar to Nova's. One of my escorts shoves me into the ring, the magic stinging my skin. The crowd closes in around the edges, jittering with cruel excitement. I turn and link eyes with Nova, who watches me steadily, their face blank so I can't quite get a read on them.

The crowd behind me roars and I turn to see Hammon entering the opposite end of the ring, chest bare. He grins, looking at the silvery moon above us.

"It's almost at its peak," he sneers, looking to me. "Don't worry. It should be over soon. Though someone did speak on your behalf, asking me to give you the option of joining me when you lose. How do you like the taste of power, Kai?"

I clench my hands into fists at my side. "I won't join you."

"Not even if it means you live?"

I shake my head. "Life as one of your pawns is no life."

Hammon's grin is cruel. "So be it." He closes his eyes and

leans his head back, the moonlight reflecting across his features. "Here it comes."

His eyes snap open and find mine. There's nothing human about them. There's not even anything natural about them at all. His irises have transformed to a sickening yellow and his pupils are ink-black slits. His lips turn up into a wolfish grin, revealing rows of jagged teeth. He throws his head back and a howl escapes as his body contorts. His limbs twist at painful angles, the human features disappearing in favor of gray skin covered in coarse black hair. The nails on his feet and hands grow into long, yellow claws as his thighs thicken, splitting his pants. The sickening cracking of bones echoes through the night and bile rises in my throat, my inner wolf terrified.

I almost can't control myself as I take a step back, my senses screaming at me to put distance between myself and this threat. A snarl behind me grabs my attention and I spin around to discover more of these beasts throughout the crowd. Even if I wanted to escape, I couldn't. I meet Nova's anxious gaze before turning back to the threat before me. The only way out is to win.

I reach inside and call on my wolf. It's a natural dance to pull him forward and I sink forward on familiar paws. Now that I'm in my most primal form, I can smell the full scent of the werewolf. Its stench floods my nostrils and burns my lungs.

The creature roars and lunges forward. I dodge, managing to land a quick nip on the back of his leg. This only makes him furious, and he swipes a claw my way. My reflexes as a wolf are quick, and I dodge him easily. I have spent a good chunk of my time over the past few years as a wolf, and my instincts are strong. Every time the beast comes my way, I artfully dodge him, but I'm not able to land many blows myself.

The crowd around us cheers and boos, their energy a

distracting force. I manage to block them out until I hear a familiar voice call my name. I turn to find Nova's wide, terrified eyes locked on something past me in the crowd. My heart stills when I see Eleni, pushed down on her knees, the claws of one of the other beasts on her shoulder. She has a deep gash across her left cheek.

I'm sorry, she mouths as her eyes meet mine.

There was already so much on my shoulders. This fight already had so much meaning. But now, someone else's life is directly at stake. I cannot lose.

With renewed vigor I leap into battle, snarling, my legs shaking. The beast lands a hard blow to my side, his claws digging into my flesh. I yelp and stumble away. Hammon takes advantage of my wound and lunges forward, catching my shoulder in his maw. The bite stings far worse than it should. It's only then I remember the myths claiming werewolves produce a debilitating venom, realizing they must be true. When he pulls back, I falter, fighting against the numbness threatening to shut down what bit of control I have.

The beast's mouth turns into what could almost be considered a grin if it weren't so horrific in nature. My legs falter beneath me and the world spins. I fight the darkness threatening to close in, but it's not enough. I'm quickly fading. I'm only vaguely aware of Hammon moving closer, and I stagger away. I avoid the full power of his bite, but his teeth still snag along my skin, tearing the flesh on my side. With a whimper I fall back, hope seeping from me faster than the blood from my wound. I squeeze my eyes shut, preparing myself for my inevitable loss.

I was a fool to think I could do this alone. I need more time. I need . . . help.

Then I feel it, a reminder that I'm not alone in this fight.

It starts as a small burning in my gut and slowly spreads

outward. The potion from Eleni must be doing something to fight off the effects of the bite. It's renewing my strength enough that I'm able to rise, my vision clearing. When Hammon lunges toward me again, I'm able to move out of his grasp. I'm recovering quickly but I'm still unsteady. Hammon roars in fury and I maneuver myself so I can see him. He's suspended mid-leap by a buzzing red magic. He struggles against its hold to no avail. He's trapped. I glance to the crowd and see Nova, eyes locked on Hammon and their hands extended. Sweat beads on their forehead with the intensity of focus it takes to restrain the werewolf. They're buying me time.

I take a deep breath and it stabilizes me enough that I can fight back. Nova's magic falters, but this time when the beast charges, I'm ready. I dodge his bite but dive into him, my teeth piercing the thick flesh at his neck. He snarls, attempting to shake me off, but I remain firm, digging in deeper. His rancid blood fills my mouth, turning my stomach, but I don't loosen my grip, not even when his claws swipe at me in attempt to pull me away. Hammon staggers and I jerk the wound, more blood spilling out. His body falls with a resounding thud. I finally release my hold and step back. His unnatural eyes stare off, unfocused, and his breathing is rough and ragged. One breath. Two. Then they cease.

Shifting from my wolf form is painful, but I can't stay a wolf any longer. The wounds tear as I shift, warm magic prickling over my skin. I bend over, heaving the vile blood along with the full contents of my stomach. When I'm able to focus, I turn my attention to the chaos of the crowd around me. Half of the bystanders seem to be rejoicing or at least relieved. The other half appear to be split between fury and fear. I wonder briefly why the other werewolves and shifters haven't attacked me in my weakened state as revenge for their leader when I realize that the warm magic wrapping me is the transfer of their blood oaths.

I swallow hard and look to where Nova stood earlier, but they're not there. I frantically scan the crowd until I spot them on the ground not far away, their body covered in blood and their breathing shallow. Above them stands a wolf, not a were-wolf, but a Hammon-loyal wolf all the same, its mouth covered in Nova's blood.

"Stop!" I yell. "Get away from them!"

Even as the command leaves my mouth, I can taste the weight of it, bitter and harsh. The wolf twitches, jerking away from Nova as if pulled by an invisible leash. It snarls and snaps its teeth, but it makes no move to harm me or Nova. I rush to Nova's side and pull them into my lap.

"I need a Healer!" I yell, looking desperately up at the crowd that surrounds me. "Fetch me a Healer!"

Someone in the crowd darts away and I turn my focus to the friend in my lap.

"You did it," Nova whispers, their words garbled with blood.

"I had help. *Your* help. And I need you to stick around a bit so we can celebrate. Okay? Promise me that you'll hang on."

Nova manages a weak smile, their teeth covered in blood. "I don't make promises I can't keep."

The words sting, as I'm sure they're meant to, but I can't focus on me right now. Nova is all that matters. A figure kneels next to me. I know without turning toward her that Eleni has joined my side. Thank the gods she survived as well.

"Try this," she says, holding out her hand to offer me a small vile filled with a black liquid.

"What is it?" I ask, taking the bottle, already working to remove the cork.

"It's similar to what I gave you to fight the effects of the poison. It will speed up the healing process."

With a grateful nod, I tip the contents into Nova's mouth. They sputter but manage to down most of the liquid. Their eyes close and I fear each breath will be their last.

"How long does it take to work?"

Eleni shrugs. "I'm not sure. I've never had to use it with wounds this severe."

A coughing fit overtakes Nova and I clutch them tightly, pulling them snuggly against my chest.

"You're going to be okay," I whisper, resting my chin on their head. "You have to be okay. Please be okay."

They sputter again and inhale sharply. The breath rattles their lungs but when they take a second breath it sounds more stable. The crowd parts and a young girl with wide eyes kneels on the other side of Nova.

"Are you a Healer?" I ask.

The girl blinks at me, trembling. Before I can repeat my words, Eleni says something rapidly in a different dialect. The girl nods.

"She is a Healer," Eleni confirms.

The girl says something softly and Eleni nods, turning to me.

"She needs to see their wounds."

I slowly relax my arms, keeping Nova securely in my lap but allowing the Healer access. She assesses Nova for a moment before extending her hands over them. A soft glow radiates from her palms and Nova gasps, their eyes shooting open. I swallow hard and let the Healer work. I can't see many of the wounds hidden by Nova's blood-soaked clothes, but I can tell most of them are closing. Nova's eyes close as the magic passes over them and their chest rises and falls with sleep. After a few minutes, the Healer falls back, someone behind her catching her. She offers me a soft smile and whispers something. I look to Eleni who also smiles.

"She says they will be okay."

Tears well in my eyes and I pull Nova into a tight hug, pressing a kiss to their head.

"I'm glad your friend is healed," Eleni says, leaning in, "but we do have pressing matters at hand."

It's only then I allow my attention to be drawn back to the restless crowd. I look to Eleni.

"What do I do now?"

"I would start by demanding that anyone under the blood oaths remain here to be counted. You want to rein in Hammon's strongest supporters before they can get away. Then you need to get to a Healer yourself."

I nod and glance down at Nova.

"I will take your friend and care for them," she says. "You go lead your new pack."

Her words pour over me like ice and my breath catches in my throat.

"Now is not the time for fear, wolf. It is the time for courage. You have won. Now lead."

NINE

It's bordering on winter, but you wouldn't know it today —not until the wind blows, that is. The sun is shining in full force, its rays warming the earth. Leyana and I have lived in the Valley for two years now, and no place has ever felt more like home. We're happy here. We're content.

As I stroll toward the dining hall, I hear Leyana's bright laugh before she comes into view. She's with her typical cluster of companions, her arm linked with Jaila, her closest friend. On her left, Jaila's older brother, Myat, blushes furiously while Jaila, Leyana, and the other three accompanying them laugh. I hide my own grin as they approach.

"Did you enjoy your morning guard duty?" Leyana asks brightly, pulling away from her group and stopping in front of me.

When a guard position opened recently, I was more than happy to leave the kitchen behind and accept the change in assignment. Follik agreed it was much more natural for a wolf shifter to be a guard than part of the kitchen staff.

"I suppose. It's much more enjoyable to be outdoors than it was to be locked in the kitchens."

"So, you're not sick of the outdoors?" she asks, a mischievous glint in her eye.

I chuckle. "I doubt I'll ever be sick of the outdoors."

She grins, bouncing on the balls of her feet. I know what she's about to ask even before the words leave her mouth. "Do you want to go for a run in the woods after you eat lunch?"

"I would love nothing more." I glance past Leyana to her friends. "As long as it wouldn't interrupt your day."

Leyana shrugs. "Not really. We just finished eating and were walking Myat to the Healing station to start his work. After that I'm free."

"All right, then. Meet you in our usual spot in about fifteen minutes?"

Leyana nods eagerly. "See you then."

Leyana prances off with her friends, their lively conversation starting up immediately. I head inside the dining hall and grab some lunch. Since it's toward the end of the lunch hour, I'm able to secure my food quickly and I arrive before Leyana. We always meet in the same spot—that small cliff overlooking the Valley. The view never fails to take my breath away.

"You beat me!"

I turn around to a grinning Leyana and I can't help but match her grin.

"Just a reminder that I'll always be one step ahead."

"Mm-hm. Whatever you want to think, dearest brother."

"Oh, I don't think. I know. Like I know that Myat is clearly interested in pursuing a relationship with you."

Color floods Leyana's cheeks. "Wha— Why would you say that? He's just a friend."

"And you don't think he might want more?"

"I—" She hesitates, glancing down. "He may have recently

mentioned becoming more than friends." She looks back up at me with a scowl. "But I don't want to talk about that."

"Fine, but you are the one always going on about the importance of a pack."

She crosses her arms, pursing her lips. "I'm always trying to convince *you* to expand your circle of friends. Hell, Kai, I'd be happy if you'd make just one friend."

I wave her off. "I have friends."

"You have acquaintances and people you work shifts with. A true pack—"

"—is a trusted group of close friends that are an extension of your family," I finish for her. "I know, Leyana. You made me read all the books about shifters, too."

"A wolf shifter without a pack is just a wolf. They need a pack to keep them human."

"If I recall correctly, your books said that a pack can consist of two wolves. I have you. You're my pack. You can keep me human."

Leyana rolls her eyes. "Come on, Kai. You need more than just me."

"I don't, Ley."

"What if something happens to me?"

I take a step closer to her. "Nothing will ever happen to you. I won't let it."

"You can't always be there, Kai."

I place my hands on her shoulders and meet her eyes. "Leyana, I will always protect you. I have lost too much in my life, and I will not lose you."

"But Kai," she protests, her voice so quiet it would be lost to sounds of the forest if she weren't so close, "just in case something does happen—gods forbid—I need to know you'd be okay. You need a pack."

"If I lose you, Leyana, I won't even want to be here, let

alone be part of a pack. I will simply become a lone wolf. If the gods decide that is not the path for me, I am sure they will let me know."

She opens her mouth to protest, but I shake my head and she falls silent.

"Enough melancholy. We came up here to run, not to argue."

She smiles, but it's weak. "All right, but don't think I'm not bringing this up later."

I shake my head affectionately but don't fight her, taking a step back.

"See if you can keep up," she says, shifting and running off immediately.

I quickly follow suit, following her trail. Together we race through the trees. Technically, I'm the faster of the two of us, but she's more nimble, able to artfully dodge through the underbrush with more ease than I can. I'm so focused on catching up to her, I don't realize how close we are to the magical borders until it's too late.

Something in me jerks uncomfortably. It's not painful, but it's a strong enough sensation that the breath is pulled from my lungs. I stagger, my vision blurring. I haven't left the Valley in two years. Magic has been so much a part of me, it's as familiar as breathing. Without it prickling across my skin, I feel like I'm missing a key sense.

I frantically search for Leyana. Usually when we're in our wolf forms, we can communicate in a unique way. It's not so much words as it is feelings, but without magic coursing through me, I come up empty. I can't sense her at all. Panic twists in my gut. I need to find her.

I leap through the trees, searching desperately. It takes me a moment to realize that even if my magical senses are shut down, I still have my heightened wolf senses. I pause, raising my muzzle to sniff the air. I catch Leyana's familiar scent, but the comfort at realizing she's not far is short-lived. Her scent isn't the only one I catch on the wind. The scent of unfamiliar humans floods my veins with fear. I race after the trail and am nearing Leyana when I hear her yelp.

My heart plummets into my stomach as I rush over the uneven terrain. I break through some trees and find myself looking down into a clearing where Leyana faces off against four hunters, an arrow sticking from her side. She snarls and lunges toward one of the hunters, grabbing his wrist. An arrow shoots from the tree cover to my left, joining the first arrow. She cries out in pain and falls. Anger surges through me and I leap from the trees. I find the hunter who shot the arrow, not even hesitating to jump on him and tear out his throat. The hunters behind me call out and an arrow shoots my way but misses. I turn my focus to the remaining hunters who are now on full alert. I run toward them, dodging an arrow. Blood floods my mouth as I tear into another hunter. Leyana struggles to her feet and joins me long enough to help me take out a hunter before a third arrow strikes her.

I look to our right and spot a sixth hunter half-hidden in the trees, his eyes wide with terror. He loads another arrow meant for me as I rush toward him. His hands shake, making his aim unsteady. The arrow sails through the air, lodging in my back leg, but it doesn't slow me. His scream is garbled by blood as my teeth lock around his throat and tear. When I turn back to the other hunters, they're already fleeing through the trees. I start to chase after them, but Leyana whimpers, drawing my attention. I bound to her side.

Her breathing is shallow and her coat wet crimson. She needs a Healer now, but I can't wisp. Not from here. I brush her cheek with my muzzle, doing my best to let her know I'll be right back. I race toward the magical border, but my wounded leg interferes with my speed. Every second feels like an eternity.

The moment I feel the warmth of magic cascade over me, I'm shifting. The arrow in my leg dislodges in the shift, but I'm even more unstable with the wound in my human form than I was as a wolf. As a human, my senses are sharper than average, but they aren't as strong as when I'm a wolf. I'm disoriented and unfamiliar with this part of the woods. It's only by spotting my trail of blood that I'm able to find my way back to Leyana.

At first I think I'm too late. Her breathing is so slow it's almost nonexistent. And there is so much blood. She takes a shaky breath and blinks up at me with her blue-gray eyes. She doesn't have long. I scoop her, nearly losing my balance thanks to my wounded leg.

"Hang on, Ley," I whisper, my voice trembling. "Just hang on. I'll get you home. We'll find a Healer. You'll be okay. You *have* to be okay."

She's heavy and awkward in my arms, but my determination drives me forward as I stumble through the trees. When I pass back over the magical border, the power of the magic pulses over me and I fall, Leyana tumbling from my arms. I reach to scoop her back up, but before I can she takes a deep breath, shifting back into her human form.

"Ley!" I cry out, pulling her into my lap.

She looks up at me and manages a small smile. She mumbles something slurred and overall incoherent but my panicked brain can only make out the word "pack." Then her eyes shutter closed. I wait a moment for them to open again, but they don't. She's gone entirely still in my arms.

"No! Wake up!" I give her a shake as tears well in my eyes. "Hang on, Ley. Please. Hang on."

I take a deep breath, reaching into my magic to wisp. My

body is drained from my recent shifting while wounded and from the blood I'm still losing. It takes three attempts before I'm able to successfully wisp both of us outside the Healing rooms.

"I need help!" I cry as I push through the door, Leyana cradled against my chest.

The main Healer sits at a table in the corner, sorting jars of medicine. Her head jerks up at my entrance and her eyes widen when they fall on Leyana. She jumps from her seat.

"Place her here," she instructs, motioning to an examination table in the center of the room.

I place Leyana on the table and the Healer rolls up her sleeves.

"What happened?" she asks extending her hands over Leyana, palms facing down.

"Hunters. In the woods. They were just past the magical border. We accidentally crossed." I look from Leyana's too still body to the Healer. "Will she be okay?"

The Healer frowns.

"She has to be okay. You have to help her."

The Healer raises her eyes to meet mine and everything about the sympathy and pity in her expression has me backing away from the table, shaking my head.

"No. She can't be— You have to—"

"Kai," she says softly.

"No. No!" I yell. I clench my shaking hands into fists and squeeze my eyes shut. "No!"

"What's going on?"

My eyes snap open as Myat steps from the back room, freshly cut bandages in his arms. He frowns as his gaze falls on me.

"Kai? Are you okay? What are you—"

He stops short with a gasp when he spots Leyana's blood-soaked body on the table. The bandages tumble from his arms as his hands fly to cover his mouth. He looks from Leyana to me, tears flooding his eyes.

"Is she okay?" He looks to the Healer. "Can you save her? Please, save her."

"I'm sorry," the Healer says, her voice gentle. "There's nothing I can do. She's gone."

A sob chokes out of Myat as I crumple to the ground, my world closing in on me. It's only thanks to the pain radiating from my wound that I remember the arrow I took, but I can't make myself care. I hope the wound kills me.

The Healer, however, has a different idea. I'm vaguely aware of her hands gripping my wound as warm magic pours over me. She says something, but I can't register the words. A moment later a cool vial is tipped against my lips and I swallow the bitter liquid on instinct. I welcome the darkness as it closes in. Anything is better than feeling. Anything is better than knowing I'm alone.

TEN

"You need to stop hiding in this gods forsaken office," Eleni says as she throws the door open and strolls inside like this is her office and not mine.

I frown at her. "I'm not hiding." I glance at the door she's left wide open. "Close that."

She arches an eyebrow. "Afraid someone will find you?"

I glare in response and nod sharply at the door.

"Hiding," she insists, closing the door anyway.

"I don't mean to hide," I admit. "I need a break from everyone, though. They keep looking to me for answers I don't have."

"That's because they're your new pack," Eleni replies, stepping up to my desk and looking down at me.

"They're not my—"

"Yes they are. They are literally blood-bound to you, like it or not. Now"—she reaches into her pocket, pulling out a slip of paper—"I have an updated count of how many people here are blood-sworn to you."

She drops the list on my desk and I scoop it up. I frown at the paper.

"Am I actually supposed to be able to read your handwriting? This is atrocious."

She rolls her eyes, crossing her arms. "If you don't like my handwriting, do it yourself."

I sigh and scan the paper. Shifters are listed first. Apparently we have 167 shifters broken down into wolves, birds, and assorted four-legged animals. Wolves account for the majority. We have around fifty or so people with elemental magic, a couple dozen with some sort of attack specific magic, nine Healers, two Seers, and around a hundred more with assorted magic. There are also dozens of non-magical people who were tricked into blood oaths for one reason or another and a few more that aren't attached by oaths but are still sticking around to support loved ones. All in all, we have a few hundred people that I'm suddenly in charge of and, according to additional notes scribbled in the margin, most are willing to travel to Callenia if the queen gives the okay.

Someone knocks on the door and I glance up at Eleni, raising a questioning eyebrow. She shrugs.

"You need a new hiding spot. People know you're here."

I shake my head. "I'm not hiding." The person knocks again. "Can you get that?"

"Yes, boss."

"Don't call me that."

"Whatever you say . . . boss."

I growl at her but she only grins as she opens the door. Of everyone who might have sought me out, I was not expecting Nova. They've been avoiding me ever since they healed enough to leave their bed. I quickly stand to my feet and Eleni eyes me curiously as Nova looks down, avoiding my eyes. I clear my throat and try to regain my composure.

"What can I do for you?"

Nova glances up quickly before looking away again. "There's an army captain asking for you. Says he's from the queen."

"Oh, yeah, by the way, boss," Eleni says, picking at her nails, "I saw a small army approaching earlier."

"Seriously, Eleni? You couldn't have given me a heads up?"

She shrugs. "I forgot."

"Should I show him in?" Nova asks hesitantly.

"Yes, please."

Nova leaves, casting me one last glance before the door shuts.

"What exactly is your history?" Eleni asks, leaning on the desk and staring up at me. "I keep trying to figure out if you two were lovers at some point."

I roll my eyes as I sit back down. "We were never lovers. I've never been interested in anyone in that way."

"Never?"

"Never. I would appreciate it if you would believe me and stop asking."

"Very well," she says, pushing up from the desk. "I respect that. I won't ask again, but there is *something* there between you."

"We were very good friends." I sigh and run a hand through my hair. "We were quite close, and I messed that up."

Eleni perches on the edge of my desk. "How so?"

I swat at her. "Get off my desk."

She rolls her eyes but complies. "How did you mess that up?"

"It's complicated, but I didn't keep a promise. I failed them."

"And now you want to fix it?"

I nod. Eleni tilts her head, studying me.

"You know, I think I had you pegged wrong."

"What do you mean?"

"When we first met, I thought you were a lone wolf."

I scowl. "You knew I was here on behalf of people from Callenia."

"Yeah, yeah." She waves me off. "I thought you felt more indebted to them, or at the very least, it was a recent development that forced you into a pack situation. I figured despite those attachments that you were a lone wolf at your core."

"But you don't think that anymore?"

She shakes her head. "No, you're not a lone wolf. You're a stray."

I scoff. "That sounds derogatory."

"I don't mean it in a bad way," she says quickly. "I just mean that . . . How do I describe this? You seemed okay being alone. Even convinced yourself that's what you wanted."

"It was what I wanted."

"No, you didn't realize it, but you wanted a pack. Needed one. I know you hate that all these people are blood-bound to you, but I've seen how you handle them. I see how you react to Nova. I've heard you talk about Astra and Ehren and Alak. You care, Kai. You don't really want to go back to being alone."

"It's easier that way."

She nods. "Yeah, it is. That's why I've been alone. It's easier when people don't depend on you. You can't fail them that way, and they can't fail you. There are no expectations. You lost your pack at some point, I'm assuming. You thought that made you a lone wolf, but it doesn't. You've just been wandering, waiting for your new pack to reveal itself. You've been a stray wolf, looking for a home, waiting for the day a new pack accepts you."

As much as I hate it, her words make sense, but I'm not ready to admit that quite yet.

"What about you? Do you still claim to be a lone wolf? After all, you did return to help me fight and you're still sticking around."

She hesitates, shifting uncomfortably. "I'm not sure, but you might have a point."

I raise an eyebrow. "Oh?"

"In fact," she continues, "I think I may want to call in that favor you owe me."

"Already? I figured you'd hold that over me for years."

She grins, her eyes shining. "That *was* my intent but . . ."

She sobers, glancing off.

"Well?" I press. "What is your favor?"

"Take me with you," she blurts out. "When you go back to Callenia, take me with you."

I furrow my brow, staring at Eleni like she's a puzzle I need to solve. "You really want to come with me?"

She nods, licking her lips. "Will you let me?"

I pause, considering her request before I nod slowly. "Okay."

Her eyes widen. "Okay?"

"Yes. When I leave here and head back to Callenia, you can come with me."

I'm about to add a few caveats and details to my fulfillment of her request, but I'm interrupted by a knock on the door.

"Come in!" Eleni calls out and I glare at her.

Nova opens the door and a tall man in a regal captain's uniform storms into the room. Nova seems disgruntled with the man as they close the door behind them. I rise and offer the captain a salute.

"You are Kai?" he asks, eyeing me.

"I am."

He considers me for a moment before nodding. He reaches into the pack at his side and withdraws a letter, handing it to me. I accept it and look down to find the queen's official seal looking up at me.

"Queen Khristiana requested I deliver that in person. I am to wait until you have read it and follow what orders I am given."

"Very well," I say, cracking the seal as I sink into my chair. "Give me a moment."

Dear Kai,

Word of your success has reached me. I wanted to first congratulate you on doing what no one else could do. It speaks well of yourself and of your friends back in Callenia.

As per our agreement, I will provide soldiers to support your cause. I have sent Captain Langdon with a regiment of 150 soldiers. While this number may seem small, I believe the pack you freed was sworn to Hammon through highly questionable magics and you are now in possession of their oaths. In taking down Hammon, their oaths transferred to you. If this information is correct, I accept that these individuals are now yours to command. If you wish to use them to fight in your war, I will allow it if they so choose that path.

In addition to providing you with soldiers and guidance in building your army, Captain Langdon will also assist you in transferring any prisoners in your possession to a secure facility to serve punishment for their crimes.

Please, let me know if you require any further information or assistance.

Queen Khristiana

When I raise my eyes from the page, I find Captain Langdon watching me carefully.

"Do you have any questions?" he asks.

I shake my head. "I do not believe so."

"And the queen's information is correct?"

"Unfortunately." I sigh and set the letter on my desk. "The pack was blood-sworn to Hammon and their oaths transferred to me. I will not force anyone to fight in the war, but I will take command of those that choose to willingly go."

Captain Langdon nods. "And your prisoners?"

I look to Eleni and she steps forward.

"I can help you with that."

The captain cocks an eyebrow. "And you are?"

Eleni grins in a way that has me answering for her before she can say something inappropriate.

"She's my second in command."

The captain looks at me like I'm insane while Eleni beams at me. The truth is over the past week, Eleni's help has been invaluable. She stepped up in a way I didn't expect and I can't imagine trying any of this without her. Plus, if she's coming with me to Callenia, I might as well keep her close so she can't cause too much trouble.

"She has a good grasp on what has been going on," I explain. "She's been taking inventory and helping me keep everything organized."

His gaze flicks between me and Eleni for a moment before he nods in resignation. "So be it."

Eleni marches past him and flings the door open, offering him a mock salute as he passes by. She glances at me and I mouth a quick *behave*. She winks and follows the captain out, closing the door behind her.

"I should probably go, too," Nova says, startling me. I had forgotten they were in the room.

"Nova, wait," I say, standing as their hand touches the door handle.

Nova hesitates, hand still outstretched, but they don't turn to face me.

"Nova, can we talk?"

"About what?"

I take a deep breath. "Are you sticking around?"

Nova's shoulders drop and they turn slowly.

"Do I have a choice?" Their expression is overall calm, but there's something challenging in their eyes and the set of their jaw.

"Of course you do. I would never force you or anyone else to go against your personal wishes. If you want nothing to do with me ever again, you are welcome to vanish in the wind. Is that what you want?"

Nova watches me carefully, their expression masked. They open their mouth only to close it a second later. I move out from behind my desk and stop a few inches away.

"Nova, I know I screwed up. I should have stayed in touch. You tried to keep the communication open and I failed you."

"You didn't fail me," Nova says weakly.

"No, I did. I failed you. I was careless and caught up in everything that was happening in the Valley."

Nova shrugs, glancing to the side. "You had a new life that I wasn't part of. A better life. I can't hold that against you." They look back at me and meet my eyes. "I felt rejected, yes, but I didn't handle it well. I knew joining Hammon was a mistake almost as soon as I swore the oath, and I was looking for someone to blame. You were a convenient scapegoat."

"So, will you stay?"

The corner of their mouth tuns up slightly. "If you'll have me."

I smile. "I wouldn't have it any other way. I've missed you. So much."

Nova smiles softly with warm affection. "I missed you, too, and I'm glad you finally found your way back."

I start to reply, wanting to tell Nova I'm also glad I found my way back, but I pause, my brow furrowing. Nova frowns.

"What? Change your mind already?" They attempt to keep their tone light and joking, but I know them well enough to catch the genuine concern in their voice.

I huff a laugh, shaking my head. "I was just thinking."

"Oh, that's dangerous."

Their words pull a full laugh from me and Nova grins, their eyes shining.

"I was thinking," I repeat, "that I'll need someone to stay here. Not everyone who was under the blood oaths is present. Several people have shown up over the past week, but more are on the way. Would you be willing to stay here as they gather while I take the rest to Callenia? I'll make sure to stay in contact for certain this time."

Nova nods. "Of course. When will you leave?"

"Hopefully within the next couple of days."

"Do you know the path you'll take? I have a few maps I could share."

"Eleni and I planned out the route through the mountains. It should only take us a few days to get there and a couple more to reach the Summer Palace in Callenia. Hopefully we won't be too late to make a difference. However, I would appreciate your input. You have more insight on the subject."

Nova inhales slowly. "And you trust me? Despite everything?"

"If you trust me to stay in contact when I broke that promise before, then I think it's only fair I be willing to trust you. We have more good in our history than bad."

Nova's smile returns. "Thanks, Kai." They pause before asking, "Will you return after the war? Assuming we survive?"

I hesitate. Will I return? I think of Astra's laugh and smile, of the casual way Alak jokes. I think of Bram's scowl and

Ehren's smile. I even have good memories of Sama, Nyco, and Cal. I've felt more at home with them than I have with anyone else in a long time. I feel pulled to them. But now I'm also connected to the pack here in Paravlia. Even though they're new, I don't know that I can leave them, even if I wanted to.

"Do you want me to return?"

Nova holds my gaze for a moment before they nod. "If it's what you want."

My mouth turns up at the corners. "I think I might, though I don't know if I'll return immediately. I have things I'll have to take care of, but I won't abandon you, Nova." I reach out and take their hand. "I swear. If I decide not to return, I'll let you know. And if you wish to join me this time in my new life, I'll welcome you. Maybe when it's all said and done, you and I can explore the world together, make some of your maps from firsthand experience."

Nova's smile lights up their entire face, making their eyes shine like diamonds. "I would really like that, Kai." They glance over their shoulder at the door. "Well, I should go take care of some things."

"We can talk later."

"I look forward to it."

After Nova leaves, I lean back against my desk. I have no idea what I'm getting into, but I don't regret it one bit. I think back to Eleni's words when she said I was a stray and not a lone wolf. In this moment, I believe wholeheartedly that she's right. When I lost Leyana, I thought my world had ended, and in some ways it did. But now everything is starting fresh, and for the first time in years, I'm looking forward to the future.

ACKNOWLEDGMENTS

Um, thank you and stuff. Good to know that I have a pack helping me out with this whole publishing thing because there is no way I could do it all alone. My pack for this project included:

- Andi, my editor—You have super powers and don't let anyone tell you otherwise.
- My beta readers Megan, Shanti, and Mandy—Ya'll survived the trial version of this story and that's really saying something. Bravo.
- Lana, my alpha reader—You led the pack and suffered through those early drafts. I really should name a character after you . . . Well, you know and I know, so that's all that matters, right?
- Ben, my partner and artist—You put up with me and all my demands and still haven't run away. You deserve an award.
- Addie, my daughter—You helped me come up with the title and also drew some amazing artwork to go along with my story. Reach for your dreams. They're worth achieving.
- Purrsephone and River, my cats—Honestly, y'all weren't really that helpful, but with the way you kept hovering around me you sure seemed to think you were important. Purrsephone did have a

tendency to lie on top of me so I couldn't easily move which kept me in place and working, so I guess I should show her some gratitude. (Or should I say cattitude?)

- My readers—Yes, all of you, even you there in the back. Whether you just discovered this series or have been with me from the beginning, thank you so much. You really keep me going.
- Everyone else—If I haven't mentioned you yet and you think I should have, um, thanks? I mean, thank you. I couldn't have done this without you.

ABOUT THE AUTHOR

AMBER D. LEWIS is a new adult fantasy author with a Bachelor's Degree in Publishing. She currently lives in Taylors, SC with her partner and three kids. When she's not reading or writing books, you'll probably find her wandering the aisles of Target.

The Fire and Starlight Saga is Amber's first series, though she plans to write many more.

facebook.com/amberdlewisofficialauthorpage

instagram.com/mugshots_n_bookthoughts

bookbub.com/profile/amber-d-lewis